The Slippery Step

ALSO BY RAE FOLEY

Put Out the Light
Where Helen Lies
The Barclay Place
The Dark Hill
The Brownstone House
One O'Clock at the Gotham
Reckless Lady
Trust a Woman?
The First Mrs. Winston
Sleep Without Morning
Ominous Star
This Women Wanted
A Calculated Risk
Girl on a High Wire
No Hiding Place
Nightmare House
Malice Domestic
The Shelton Conspiracy
Fear of a Stranger
Scared to Death
Wild Night
Call It Accident
Fatal Lady
Repent at Leisure
Back Door to Death
It's Murder, Mr. Porter
Dangerous to Me
Where Is Mary Bostwick?
Run for Your Life
The Last Gamble
Death and Mr. Porter
Dark Intent
The Man in the Shadow
Wake the Sleeping Wolf
An Ape in Velvet
The Hundredth Door
Bones of Contention

The Slippery Step

A NOVEL OF SUSPENSE

by RAE FOLEY

DODD, MEAD & COMPANY / NEW YORK

Copyright © 1977 by Rae Foley
All rights reserved
No part of this book may be reproduced in any form
without permission in writing from the publisher
Printed in the United States of America
by The Haddon Craftsmen, Inc., Scranton, Penna.

1 2 3 4 5 6 7 8 9 10

Library of Congress Cataloging in Publication Data

The slippery step.

(A Red badge novel of suspense)
I. Title.
PZ3.D426Sm [PS3554.E56] 813'.5'4 77–23321
ISBN 0–396–07404–9

*For Lillian Gerber
in token of loyalty over
and beyond the call of duty*

The Slippery Step

1

THERE WAS no car in the slot reserved for room 12 in the underground parking lot of the motel so the maid, after checking to make sure there was no DO NOT DISTURB sign, unlocked the door and went in. It was ten-thirty and she was already behind in her work. The obstreperous couples in rooms 6 and 7 had spent a riotous night until the desk clerk had relayed complaints from irate people, and this morning, as might be expected, the rooms were a mess.

Room 12 was dark and the maid switched on the light and then stepped back hastily, muttering, "Sorry. I thought no one was here."

The girl on the bed did not move; shoulder-length hair hung over the side. So, the maid realized, did the girl's head. But you couldn't possibly sleep in that position, she thought, with your head hanging backwards like that. You couldn't—

"Hi," she said uncertainly. When there was no response, she moved slowly, reluctantly, toward the bed. "Hi," she repeated louder.

The blond hair was matted with dried blood that had seeped from a small hole in the temple. The open eyes stared at her unseeingly. The jaw hung open, revealing perfect teeth. There was a faint darkening along the jaw and the upper lip. It was not a girl but a man, a young man, who lay there, sleeping his last sleep.

Mary Roberts had grown up in a tough section of Brooklyn and she had been employed by a Manhattan motel for ten years. Like Timberlake, she had outlived surprise. She stood still for a moment, her breath coming quickly, the room developing a tendency to revolve around her; then she steadied herself, drew a long breath, and backed out, locking the door behind her.

The housekeeper, like Mary, had been seasoned in the hotel business. She listened intently and without exclamations, and then called the manager. When he had used the master key to see for himself, he gloomily called the police and then searched his records. Mr. and Mrs. Carl Lamb had checked into the motel the night before. Lamb, in accordance with house policy, had paid in advance, flashing a billfold stuffed with new hundred-dollar bills. His car had a New York license, which the night desk man had gone down to the parking lot to check out for himself.

A prowl car came first and put in a call for the Homicide boys, who arrived soon after, with a minimum of fuss and noise. Fortunately, and the only bright spot for the harassed manager, checkout time was eleven and nearly everyone had left the motel before the police invasion.

There was no mystery about the cause of death. The young man had been struck on the temple by an undetermined instrument that had a sharp point.

"He probably," the police doctor said briskly, "never knew what hit him. Of course, I'll be able to tell you more after the autopsy, but I don't think you need look farther for the cause of death . . . Time? Not less than six, not more than nine hours."

"Between one-thirty and four-thirty this morning." Forman, the detective in charge, looked automatically at his watch. He was a big man, a square man, with a wide flat face and a thin jutting nose. Mouth and eyes had been trained by years of police work to betray little, to trust little.

"Poor devil." The doctor looked down at the victim, who was unperturbed by the fuss and stir around him, the flashbulbs as pictures were shot, the taking of fingerprints from long shapely hands whose texture indicated that he had done no hard physical work. Twenty-five probably. Good-looking. Too good-looking for his own good. This should be an easy one. Find the missing Mrs. Carl Lamb, check on the car license.

"We've done that," Forman said wearily, the professional cutting short unwelcome amateur advice. "A drive-it-yourself deal, picked up late yesterday afternoon by one Carl Lamb and paid for in cash. They remembered the transaction because he pulled out a wallet filled with what looked like nice crisp new hundred-dollar bills."

"He sure seems to have carried around a lot of cash," Sergeant Purcell commented. "Usually it's credit cards or traveler's checks. Where's his wallet?"

But there was no wallet, there were no papers in the pockets of the well-tailored sports jacket from which the tailor's name and address had been removed, no keys in the pockets of the slacks. No name anywhere.

"Mr. Anonymous," Forman said. "If he was really Carl Lamb, there'd be no point in removing all identification. Someone sure as hell was careful to leave no hint as to who this guy was."

"Look for the lady," the doctor advised him and grinned at the detective's ill-concealed disgust. "Sure, sure. You know your own business best, but when you are trying to get an identification, take a tip from the old man. Don't show him as he is now. Let the experts work on him so you'll have a picture people will recognize and the media will be willing to reproduce."

"But how she managed to land a blow like that on a healthy-looking specimen is what I can't make out," Forman said.

"Chances are he was asleep. He'd been drinking. Can't you smell the gin?"

"There's a bowl of melting ice," a policeman reported, "and four glasses, two of them still in those plastic wraps. The other two—"

"Don't tell me. They've been washed. This murderer was methodical. That's one thing we know about her. Cool as they come. Took her time. Checked the guy's clothes, removed all identification and all fingerprints. And that's more of a trick than you may realize. Even the pros are apt to overlook something like the handle of a drawer, the telephone, the things you touch all the time so that they become routine and you're not aware of them. There's not a single fingerprint in the bathroom, on the television set, on the chairs or table or light switches, except the one at the door, and the maid left that. We've checked her out."

"Maybe something will come through on his prints," Sergeant Purcell said not unhopefully. He was still young enough to believe that in the long run things are bound to come out all right, an unsullied state of mind Forman regarded with some perplexity because the man was no fool. "He may have a record somewhere."

"What's your guess?" the doctor asked curiously.

Purcell was not a man to put himself forward, not at least, in the presence of his superior in rank. He glanced at Forman, who looked down at the young man with the shoulder-length blond hair, the oval face with even features marred by the gaping jaw, the wound in the temple, the wide-open sightless eyes, the blood-matted hair.

"Conning women. Selling fake stocks to widows. Blackmail. And he must have made a collection recently. He seems to have been loaded."

"Was the woman with him when he rented the car?"

"If she was, no one noticed her. Of course, we've only talked to the renting agency by telephone; we'll be seeing them personally. Jog their memories. People see a lot more than they realize. No chance of finding out here. The night clerk says he came in alone to register, which is customary, even when the relationship is legal."

The doctor yawned. "I had three calls last night and I'm half asleep."

"That's a fifty per cent improvement," Forman said without rancor.

The doctor grinned. They had bickered cheerfully for years. "Take him away. Have them pretty him up for pictures. May get an identification before I have to go to work on him."

Forman nodded. "Nothing more we can do here."

II

By early afternoon the FBI had come through with prints belonging to one Charles Lawrence, arrested two years earlier for the attempted extortion of Mrs. Harrison Fitch, widow, fifty, sole heir to the Fitch estate. Before the trial was scheduled, Mrs. Fitch had withdrawn her complaint and the police had been forced to release him.

The assistant district attorney remembered the case. "I hated to let him go. All that consoled me was knowing that this character was bound to crop up again. He was the type who thinks the idea of earning an honest living is ridiculous. Even with a couple of prison terms behind them these fellows are still convinced that they have chosen the easier way. But I didn't expect to find him here."

He looked down at the young man who lay on the slab,

his face freshly shaven, his mouth closed, long lashes sweeping the cheeks that had been faintly tinted to remove the evidences of death, a faint hint of a smile at the corners of his lips, hair washed and glossy.

"The kind who lands on his feet. A maiden's dream."

"Uh-huh," Forman retorted. "Girls don't have the kind of cash this guy wanted. Look for a ripe wealthy widow."

"Who bashed him over the head? That doesn't sound likely."

"Or you might try a ripe wealthy married woman in search of romance, and an unromantic husband who doesn't like wives with romantic ideas."

"So he persuades her to admit him in the night so he can kill the guy, and the two of them make their escape. Well, it's wide open so far. Maybe the picture will bring some action. The television people were cooperative and they'll get it on the screen with their first newscast."

"A guy like this doesn't go missing without someone wanting to find him. Find him bad," the assistant district attorney said. "It might be interesting to know whether anyone turns up here to have a look at him."

Forman nodded. "You," and he turned to Purcell, who had accompanied him to the morgue, "hang around, but not conspicuously. Just watch to see whether anyone comes to look at the guy."

Purcell looked around him in open distaste. "I stay here all afternoon?"

"If necessary. I'll get you relief by six at the latest."

"The sooner the better, as far as I am concerned. This is my least favorite spot." Purcell settled down to wait.

Hardly an hour of his uneasy vigil had passed when a young man, carrying his jacket over his arm because of the July heat, wearing a short-sleeved sport shirt, came into the morgue, spoke to the attendant and, while Purcell watched unobtrusively, waited for the drawer to be rolled out and the sheet pulled back.

The young man was of average height, wiry, with good shoulders, dark hair cut short and sternly disciplined to control a tendency to curl, and a wide puckish mouth that turned up at the corners.

When he saw the face of the man on the slab, he barely moved and yet it seemed to the watching detective as though an electric shock had coursed through his body. There was a short exchange of question and answer.

"Where did you get this?"

"A Manhattan motel. Registered with a dame who disappeared. Called himself Carl Lamb. . . . No, that's all I know, mister. Check it out with the police." The attendant rolled back the drawer, careful not to glance in Purcell's direction.

The young man nodded without replying and went out, swaying as though he was a little drunk. He did not see the detective. Probably wouldn't have seen him, Purcell thought, if he'd fallen over him. Now what was he supposed to do? Follow the guy or obey orders and stay on the job? Instinct told him that he was making the wrong decision but, with a wary eye on the unpredictable reactions of the brass, he decided to stay.

2

"THE BODY of a man," television reported at three that afternoon, "was found at a Manhattan motel this morning by a maid doing a routine room-cleaning job. The young man, who registered as Carl Lamb, was presumably accompanied by his wife. No trace of Mrs. Lamb has been found."

"The FBI," the cheerful voices from several major networks went on, "have identified his fingerprints as those of Charles Lawrence, with a record of arrest but no convictions. The police are looking for anyone who has information in regard to Lawrence and the woman who registered as his wife. If anyone was seen entering or leaving room 12 at the Regal Motel during the night, please call the following number. All information will be held strictly private."

The picture of the young blond victim was held on the screen for several seconds. He might have been asleep.

"It's a ten-to-one shot," Forman admitted. "No one is likely to come forward. Women who fell for him are apt to be afraid to testify and it's a cinch no man is going to claim him."

He was wrong. Twenty minutes later the special number was called and Forman listened in. It was not a distraught woman; it was a man so upset he was almost stuttering. "Oh, my God! Oh, my God! I don't see—and who is this Carl Lamb? And a woman with him. Chris shouldn't be in town, if it is Chris. Oh, my God! If it is, this is going to be terribly bad for my business. Children's toys, you know. Parents might be afraid—Oh, dear!"

In some dismay and with considerable reluctance he agreed to meet the detective and look at the body of the murder victim. He identified himself as Henry Toyman. "A coincidence, of course, as I manufacture toys for children. Tricks for Tiny Tots. You've probably heard of it. . . . No? Well, I guess you have no children of your own. Neither have I. Will of God, I suppose, though I've been happily married for twenty-five years. Chris is—was—my best salesman. If it was Chris. Oh, dear!"

Forman was waiting at the morgue for Toyman's arrival and he listened to Purcell's account of the young man who had looked at the body before any news had been released about it and had seemed to recognize it, though he had made no identification. Forman was about to explode when he realized the unhappy sergeant's dilemma.

"Yeah, I suppose you did the only thing possible. Could you identify the guy if he should emerge again, which I assume he won't?"

"I'd know him," Purcell said confidently. He frowned. "You know I have a feeling now that I've seen him somewhere before." He searched his memory. "No, it escapes me. But it may come back when I'm not trying to remember. You know how it is."

Forman knew how it was.

Toyman was a man of seventy, with thick bifocals, thin white hair with a wide tonsure, and the fidgety manner of the confirmed bachelor, in spite of his long marriage.

He answered Forman's patient questions in a series of nervous twitters. He had a factory and home in New Jersey whose addresses he gave. A small staff in his factory, fifteen employees, mostly women, and a minimal office staff. "Typing, you know, and billing, and orders." He said everything in a nervous way as though the process of living was too much for him and he had never quite accustomed himself to the baffling business of being a man. Chris, he said, stumbling over the name, was by far his best salesman. Terrific. A perfect dynamo. It would be a loss, a tremendous loss, but perhaps, after all, the whole thing was a dreadful mistake.

He stood for a long time after the sheet had been pulled back, looking at the quiet face with its hint of a mocking smile. At his side Forman waited for Jittery Joe, as he had named him, to collapse. But it didn't happen.

"Yes," Toyman said heavily, "that's Chris. Poor devil. And poor little Jane. This will break her heart."

"Jane?"

"His wife. They've been married only a year. What a tragedy! I don't envy you the task of breaking it to her. Unless—" He hesitated. "My wife has been like a mother to the young couple. Perhaps she could do it for you. She'd be glad to help in any way."

"Thank you. What's that name the guy called himself?"

"Christopher Lansing. His home address is on West Ninetieth Street. Oh, and about that nonsense—that story he'd been arrested on some charge under another name—that's impossible. Mistaken identity. I knew Chris like a son. Loved him like one."

Forman nodded sympathetically. "If your factory is in New Jersey, how'd you happen to get here so fast?"

"Just chance. I was in New York attending a toymakers' convention. We hold one every year, displaying our new items in preparation for Christmas sales." For the first time he smiled, almost coyly. "Oh, we have to work far in advance of the season to be jolly, you know. Keeping way ahead of Santa Claus."

He had hardly returned to his display of Tricks for Tiny

Tots when the morgue attendant reported to Forman that there was another caller on the special number.

This time it was a woman. "About that man who died—the one on television with the blond hair—there's some mistake. You've got the wrong picture. That's Chester Loring and he's my husband."

"Are you Jane?"

"Jane? No, I'm Beverly Baxter, at least I use that name when I'm modeling. I'm Mrs. Chester Loring."

"Well, well," Forman said as he put down the telephone and turned to Purcell. "Will the real Mrs. Loring or Lawrence or Lamb or Lansing please stand up?"

"How many more do you think will claim this guy?" Purcell asked. "What a man! What stamina!"

"She's on her way. The Lorings have an apartment on Irving Place."

Mrs. Chester Loring was tall and slim, with the high cheekbones and straight nose of the successful high fashion model, a long swinging walk and the kind of makeup that appears to be no makeup at all, simply an emphasis of the shape of the lips and a deepening of the eyes. She had strawberry blond hair that hung below her waist and she wore a beautifully tailored black slack suit with a blouse that matched her hair and sandals on bare feet with the toenails painted gold. She was, the detective thought, quite a dish. And he knew, without knowing why, that his wife would not like her.

She was, to his surprise, angry. "What's the idea of that story?" she demanded. "Some mix-up in pictures or someone who looks like Chester, enough to be a dead ringer." Which Forman thought was unexpectedly apt. "Chester will be burned up when he hears about this."

"Where is your husband, Mrs. Loring?"

"In Miami. I know it's a hell of a time of year to go to

11

Florida, but he has this aunt there, only relative, and loaded. Well, I mean when she gets sick or thinks she's sick and lets out a yell, Chester answers."

They had been married five months and Chester had to be away a lot, selling electronic equipment. But don't ask her what kind. None of it made sense to her.

Unlike the jittery Mr. Toyman, she agreed with alacrity to view the body. "I never thought the police were such dopes," she said, walking with her long graceful stride beside the big detective. "I'll bet Chester could bring suit against you."

She waited, looking around her curiously, while the sheet was lifted. She stared at the quiet face and her own crumpled. "Oh, no," she whispered. "Oh, no! Chester darling!"

The detective caught her as she fell.

II

"We might as well finish the thing now," Forman said. He grinned at Purcell. "Okay, you've done your stint here. Come along." He glanced at the imperturbable morgue attendant. "If you get any more candidates claiming this bird, hold them until you can give me a call. But even Don Juan here must have had a limit. That little man has been living a crowded hour and how he managed to keep his women apart is more than I can see."

They paused for a moment to breathe in gratefully the air saturated with smog, dust, dirt, and exhaust. It was heaven to be out of doors, to see people pass by, worried and anxious, hurrying toward an unknown future, but at least alive.

At Forman's nod the policeman at the wheel touched his siren and the car screamed up through Central Park and headed west, where he shut off the siren so they could approach silently.

"I've been on the force eight years," Purcell said suddenly, "and this is the first time I've been in on this."

"Breaking the news?"

The sergeant nodded and swallowed.

"It doesn't get any easier. It never gets any easier. And it's worse, of course, when it's one of our own."

"You think this is the one, that she's the guy's real wife?"

"Can you see any wife of Toyman's mothering that model? What does she call herself? Beverly Baxter, Barker, something like that."

Purcell couldn't.

The apartment building was on West Ninetieth Street in a run-down converted brownstone. The Lansings, the superintendent said, had the front basement apartment. His own quarters were at the back.

"I hope there's nothing wrong." He eyed the two men uneasily. "A nice young couple. Quiet. In love. Never any complaints."

"See the news on television at three o'clock? Probably," and Forman looked at his watch, "again on the hour."

The superintendent shook his head. "That dame on the third floor—the police in this precinct will know, they've been here before—that's what I thought you were after. Mrs. Jameson, at least that's what she calls herself, drinking again and this time dropped a cigarette on the couch. Had to get the fire department and break in the door. She's in the hospital and I suppose she hasn't a dime to pay for the wreck the place is in, couch and drapes ruined and a hole in the carpet, to say nothing of the water stains."

The two policemen braced themselves for an ordeal and went down the area steps to the basement apartment, the space cluttered with a couple of garbage cans, a child's bicycle, and a baby carriage. As one man they paused abruptly.

The window of the apartment was a bright oblong of light, and silhouetted against it was a man holding a girl in his arms.

Purcell tugged at Forman's sleeve. "The guy from the morgue," he said. "So help me, the guy from the morgue."

3

JANE LANSING lifted the heavy bag of groceries onto the small shelf, which was the only working space in her tiny kitchenette, and put the steak in the refrigerator. There was always a steak for celebration when Chris came home. She hummed to herself while she put away the vegetables and laid a bottle of Blue Nun on its side in the refrigerator. That too was for tonight. Of course, some Fridays Chris was held up and couldn't make it for the weekend, but this one was safe. She gave a little skip of sheer joy.

She looked around the apartment, unaware of her dingy surroundings, of the small, airless, cramped living-bedroom combination with the sagging couch that became a bed at night, and which had been there when they rented the apartment a year before. At that time she had been conscious of discouragement. There was nothing she could make of this, but it was all Chris could afford. He had a mother crippled by arthritis and a backward sister in upper New York State whom he visited regularly, sacrificing some of the precious weekends and helping them out of his small salary.

It was all right, she had assured him. Wait and see how she could turn the little one-room basement apartment into a home.

He had swung her up in his arms, laughing, kissing her

mouth and throat before he set her down. "Dora, my child wife."

"No," and she had been serious. "Not a child wife. I don't think I care for child wives. A real wife or nothing."

And she had done her best. She had put firmly out of her mind all of Uncle Jim's warnings, though she had hated hurting and disappointing him. Never before had she questioned his judgment, but then never before had he come down so firmly in opposition to a wish of hers.

"You're only eighteen, honey. You have no experience of men. Granted this guy is good-looking, but he's—the truth is that I don't trust him."

"Uncle Jim!" The cry was half anger, half outraged protest.

"He's too evasive. Oh, plausible as hell in a lot of ways, but what actually do you know about him?"

"I love him!"

Uncle Jim, big and broad-shouldered and beginning to be overweight, shrugged helplessly. "I can't stop you, honey. But I'd give an arm and a leg if you had never met the guy. He's bad news, Jane. Sooner or later, one of two things will happen: you'll find out what he is and suffer for it, or you'll grow to be like him."

"So?" she challenged him, standing her full five foot two, her head high.

"So you'd become a shoddy Jane. I don't want that to happen. But one thing—and I know you'll resent this—I'm holding onto your money until he can prove that he is responsible."

Jane had smiled then, a smile that set her whole face alight. "Why should I resent it? Chris won't care and I won't care. Learning how to manage on a small income will be a challenge. I'm going to love it, Uncle Jim."

And she had. Today should be the proof because it would

mark their first wedding aniversary and, except for his frequent absences as a traveling salesman in toys and his obligatory visits to his mother and sister, it had been perfect. She flung out her arms and danced across the room singing, "So in love am I."

She got out the shirt she was making as a present for Chris and switched on the radio, getting a local station. "You have just heard the news," a voice said. "Our next scheduled news will be at—" She switched to WQXR and got *Swan Lake*. While she stitched and listened to the music, she remembered how, as a very little girl, she had wanted to be a ballet dancer. As usual, Uncle Jim had indulged her and she had taken lessons for a year. Then she had wanted to be a business woman and Uncle Jim had tried to teach her accounting. In vain. He was the one who had been forced to give up his job as teacher.

"It's no use, honey. Figures don't mean a thing to you."

She had laughed and abandoned in relief her brief and bewildering introduction to mathematics. She still had to add on her fingers and did it, rather anxiously, at supermarkets while making her careful selections. One good thing about Chris's frequent absences, the only good thing, was that she could manage on canned soup and sandwiches most days, or maybe an egg and salad. The money she saved went into gold nylon curtains that shut out the barred basement window and gave the room a fictitious suggestion of sunlight. She had even found at a secondhand store a big easy chair, almost new, and had re-covered it herself rather patchily, but Chris enjoyed it and she had covered some cheap pillows with needlepoint. The room really looked very nice, she told herself firmly, and she compensated for the lack of fresh air by taking brisk walks along windy Riverside Drive.

She had been so totally happy that she had not missed her friends, none of whom lived in this unfashionable neighborhood. She had realized from the beginning that there was no point in trying to keep up with them. Chris would only be embarrassed and made to feel inadequate as a provider, though heaven knew he was carrying two men's responsibilities without complaint. In fact, his gaiety of spirit, the boyishness that made him seem younger than she, was undimmed by his grim struggle to earn a living that would provide for so many people.

She laid aside the shirt to prepare some lunch, a peanut-butter sandwich, some cottage cheese, and a glass of milk. Heavens, what milk cost! At the end of *Swan Lake* she switched off the radio. She never turned on television until evening. The midafternoon period, she admitted to herself, sometimes seemed long. Seemed empty. Perhaps she ought to get a job of some kind. She was untrained, of course, but there should be something, even unpaid, to fill those vacant hours. A volunteer in a day-care center for children, perhaps. Then when her own family came, and Chris said they could have children as soon as he got a raise, she'd know more about how to bring them up.

She reached idly for the telephone directory. What did you look under: child care? welfare? Someone ran down the basement stairs and she dropped the directory on the floor as she leaped to her feet. No one ever came here. Her friends did not know where she lived. Uncle Jim stayed away because, for her sake, he wanted to avoid any unpleasantness. Mike? But one never knew about Mike. And, of course, Chris's mother and sister never left Buffalo.

Oh, it might be Mrs. Toyman, who came occasionally to see her and give her some motherly advice about shopping and fixing up the apartment, or just talking in a comfortable way, saying encouraging things about Chris's activities, his abilities, and his bright future. But Mrs. Toyman did not run lightly downstairs. She was an overweight woman who walked ponderously. Usually she brought with her a loaf of some strange bread she had baked or some peculiar-tasting herbs that had, according to her, magical properties. For Mrs. Toyman was a food faddist. Jane always thanked her warmly and discarded these well-meant offerings when her friend had gone, laughing about them to Chris.

She opened the door before there could be a knock and cried out in astonished delight, "Mike! How wonderful. And how did you find me? Oh, Uncle Jim, of course." She caught his hand, dragging him into the room. Then she stood smiling up at him.

"You're just the same," she exclaimed. "Just the same! Oh, it's so good to see you!"

He put his hands on her shoulders, thinner than they had been a year before, and looked down into her radiant face. For a moment his hands tightened and she thought he was going to take her in his arms, but he let his hands fall.

Hey, she thought in surprise, where's that puckish smile? We might be strangers instead of best friends as well as practically cousins.

"Me Jane," she said, trying to bring back his smile by their old joke, but there was no answering smile on his face.

"Yes, Uncle Jim told me how to find you," he said heavily. "He wants me to take you home. He'll be waiting."

Jane's smile faded. "But this is my home," she reminded him gently. She saw the ripple along his jaw, saw him thrust betraying hands into his pockets. She put a hand on his arm. "What's wrong, Mike?" Because her life in recent months had been so concerned with a lack of money, she asked, "You haven't been plunging too deep in the market?"

"Oh, no. I'm still solvent. And I finally landed the job I was after, reporting for the *Chronicle.* That's how—" He broke off. Then he tried again. "Have you listened to the news this afternoon?"

She shook her head, wondering.

"One of my routine jobs, while I'm waiting for my own nationwide syndicated column," he was trying now to recapture their old jokes but he wasn't making much of a job of it, "is covering the police blotter, checking the morgue, all that." He watched her but there was no change in her face, an oval face with wide-set brown eyes, a small nose, and a lovely mouth. Not beautiful but the face he loved. He knew its every expression.

He pushed her down gently on the couch and sat beside her, aware of the broken spring that made the cushion sag. "This afternoon I dropped in at the morgue. Routine. Missing persons stuff. Sometimes the lead for a story." He turned slightly toward her, watching her profile, seeing the slight frown between her well-marked dark brows. Not shock. Only bafflement.

"A man's body had just been brought in. He's been murdered by a blow on the temple. He was found in the Regal Motel where he had registered as Carl Lamb—with a wife. There was no woman with him when the maid discovered the body."

"Mike, you aren't going to shift to crime reporting, are you? What you've always dreamed of is a column of your own. Don't give that up. You can make it. I'm sure you can make it." This kind of support she could give. She had learned with Chris how important it was to build a man's self-esteem, his confidence.

"Wait, Jane." Mike swallowed. This was hell. He didn't know how—but he had better be the one. Better than the police. He groped for her hand, held it in a crushing grip that hurt her. "Jane, that guy in the morgue—I recognized him."

"Oh, poor Mike! No wonder you were upset," she said with quick sympathy.

This was worse than he had anticipated. You'd think by now she'd have an inkling, a suspicion about what he was telling her.

"Jane—God! I don't know how to make this easy. It was Chris!"

For a moment the wide brown eyes stared at him in utter disbelief and then—she laughed.

"You know, just for a second you almost scared me! But it wasn't Chris! It couldn't be! Chris wasn't in New York last night, with or without a woman." She laughed again. "He was in Chicago. He'll be home tonight about six."

"How do you know he was in Chicago?"

"He calls me every single day at five-thirty when he has to be away. Every single day. And at five-thirty yesterday he called. Poor Mike! What an awful business for you."

But she could not cajole the upturned corners of Mike's mouth; the familiar pixie grin was absent from a mouth grown hard and strange to her.

"How do you know he was in Chicago, Jane?"

"I just told you."

"Did the call come through the operator?"

"No, he always calls direct. It's cheaper that way and we try not to be extravagant."

His eyes swept the room. "So I see."

Color blazed in her cheeks. "You needn't think I mind. Chris has a lot of responsibilities and he has a real future. His boss has no children and he is planning to retire next year. From something his wife let drop we are pretty sure he intends to turn the business over to Chris, which is just plain wonderful. We can have a house in New Jersey near the business and Chris can stay home and we can start a family. And maybe Uncle Jim will see then that Chris is responsible and let me have my own money. Not," she added hastily, "that it would matter a single scrap to Chris."

"It was Chris," Mike said. "There is no conceivable doubt about it."

The color was fading now, doubt growing, fear growing. "You can't be that sure."

"May I use your phone?"

She waved toward it, not speaking.

He called the *Chronicle,* asked for the city desk, identified himself. "Anything new on the man registered as Carl Lamb who was murdered at the Regal Motel?" He listened. He listened a long time. "What's that? Started as open-and-shut and now it's wide open. Well, they have a nice field to play around in . . . No, nothing to add. I'm with his wife now . . . Cut it out!" His voice was savage. "She's my cousin. We practically grew up together . . . Yes, her name is Jane . . . She doesn't believe me. . . . The police? Well, it's inevitable. I'll try again."

He put down the telephone. "Jane, you've got to take this on the chin. Chris has been identified by his boss, Henry Toyman. No question of doubt." He waited a moment but there was no reaction. The brown eyes were perhaps rather opaque, the lips slightly parted.

"Word has come through on his fingerprints. He is Charles Lawrence, arrested for attempted extortion of a wealthy widow who later withdrew the charges rather than submit herself to the publicity. He has also been identified as Chester Loring by a woman who claims to have married him five months ago and who had been living with him in an apartment on Irving Place—when he is home. According to her he traveled as a salesman for electronic equipment and he was in Miami last night. She is a model. She fainted when she saw him. Wouldn't believe it until she did. Obviously she is not the woman who was registered with him at the motel last night, Mrs. Carl Lamb, who has since disappeared as completely as though she had never existed. The dead man had been seen several times loaded with new hundred-dollar bills, brand-new according to witnesses. The money has disappeared too."

Jane got up then and walked to the window where she stared out blindly, seeing but unaware of the shadows of the bars against the gold curtains. Mike switched on the lights in an attempt to break through the gloom of the room now that the last glimmer of daylight was too dim to reach the single window. Then he went back to take her by the shoulders and turn her to face him. The eyes she lifted to his were tearless but might have been blind.

"It's all been a lie. Everything has been a lie. The love. The happiness. Everything I had. Everything I will ever have."

He gave her a little shake. "Hey, stop that! You're only nineteen. You haven't begun to live. There's a new day a-coming." She remained rigid, still abnormally calm, almost frozen. Somehow he had to break through that, to bring her relief. What he longed to do was to cry out his love for her, but this was no time for it, if there ever would be a time, so he put his arms around her, rocking her gently. "Uncle Jim's waiting. He wants you to come home. He needs you, Jane. He's a very lonely man."

"With all his clubs and friends and hobbies and travel?" she protested. And then she was crying, her hands clutching at his shirt, her face buried against his breast—wild sobbing that he made no attempt to check.

With his cheek resting on her soft hair, he was unaware of the two men descending the basement stairs. He started when there was a peremptory tap at the door. For a moment his arms tightened. "Darling, something unpleasant is going to happen. But you'll meet it as you've met everything. Remember the day you finished the tennis match with a sprained ankle?" He released her and she straightened her shoulders and went steadily to open the door, wiping her wet cheeks with the backs of her hands.

The big men stood looking at her. "Are you Jane Lansing?"

"I am Mrs. Christopher Lansing. Come in, won't you?" She stepped back.

Forman flashed his identification. "Detective Forman of Homicide. Sergeant Purcell."

"This is Michael Heald, my cousin, who has forestalled you in your news about my—husband. Sit down, gentlemen."

4

WHY, SHE'S just a kid, Forman thought in consternation, looking down at the small girl with the tear-stained face and the head held proudly with an effort.

"I'm sorry we have to bring you this bad news," he said with uncharacteristic gentleness. Nonetheless his eyes were alert, taking in the shabbiness of the little basement apartment, the gallant attempt to make it habitable. There weren't, he saw in relief, going to be any hysterics, or perhaps she had gone through that stage in the arms of—her cousin, was it? One thing stood out a mile. The guy, cousin or not, was in love with her. Another complication in an already complicated case.

It would be a help to know how he had happened to visit the morgue before the news story had gone out, and where he had been between one-thirty and four-thirty that morning. Probably the guy or dame who had put Lawrence, if that was his real name, out of circulation had performed a public service. Still the law was the law and Forman did not take murder lightly, even when the Mafia boys were gaily eliminating each other.

"I'll have to ask you a few questions, Mrs. Lansing."

She took a long breath, braced herself and nodded her head.

"Go easy on her," Mike said quickly. "This has been a bad shock."

"Of course. Still I'm afraid we'll have to ask you to come to the morgue."

"You've got an identification," Mike protested. "I identified him. His boss identified him. The FBI identified him. His—other wife—identified him. That should be enough."

"How do you happen to know all that?" Forman asked, and this time his voice was not gentle at all.

"I'm a legman for the *Chronicle*. Just started a few weeks ago. I dropped in at the morgue—routine—and recognized Chris."

"And it didn't occur to you to make an official identification?"

"I wanted Jane to know first. It would come easier from me."

"The morgue attendant didn't know you."

"The regular man has been out for a couple of weeks. Slipped disc or something."

The sergeant intervened. "I guess he's a reporter, all right. Thought I'd seen him somewhere before. He was in a poker game at the precinct with some other reporters. Way I remember is that he really cleaned up. Took the jackpot by sheer bluff with nothing in his hand."

Forman's brows rose. Anyone who could outbluff some hardened newsmen must have something on the beam. "Who told you that Toyman had identified the body?"

"The city desk at the *Chronicle*. They also," Mike said deliberately, "told me about the FBI identification of Chris as a man named Lawrence with a record, and a Mrs. Chester Loring's identification of him as her husband." He did not look at Jane. "And he was found in a motel room where he had registered as Carl Lamb with a wife who has since disappeared."

Jane was sitting quite still in the chair Chris had liked so much. The only sign of tension was in the fingers that plucked at the fabric, shredding the cheap material.

"When did you last see your husband?" Forman asked her.

She roused herself. "Monday morning. He left for Chicago where he sells toys. And then yesterday at five-thirty he called. He always calls at that time when he's away. He said he'd be back tonight in time for dinner." Her voice shook. "But I guess he wasn't there. He was right here in New York with this other woman who thinks she was married to him."

"No, I don't think he was with her. She claims that he was in Miami visiting a sick aunt who has the money and calls the shots. Anyhow, her shock when she saw the body was genuine."

"She—loved him too?" Jane swallowed. She was very white. Forman found himself admiring her control, but he'd seen clever actresses before, girls you'd think were too young to know the facts of life but who had records that would make your hair curl. If this wasn't all that much of a surprise to her, it changed the picture. Changed it quite a lot. Particularly with Mr. Michael Heald watchful in the background.

"He registered for Mr. and Mrs. Carl Lamb. There was no trace of a woman in the room when he was found. No fingerprints. Nothing."

"You think she—killed him and then ran away?"

"We don't know yet, Mrs. Lansing. But we will. Was—your husband in the habit of carrying a large amount of cash with him?"

Jane shook her head. "He never carried much money. We didn't have much; just enough to keep up the apartment and to enable Chris to pay most of the expenses for his crippled mother and a mentally retarded sister who live in Buffalo. He was paid three hundred dollars a month and he had an

27

expense account and made commissions on sales. His boss, Mr. Toyman, thought the world of him. Chris was the hardest worker—"

She set her lips firmly to control their quivering and stopped speaking while she steadied her voice. Mike brought her a glass of water, put it in her hand, guided it to her lips, and when she had taken a few sips he remained standing behind her chair, his hands resting lightly on her shoulders. Instinctively she leaned back against them, for comfort, for support.

Forman watched, his eyes cold. "How well do you know your husband's family?"

"I've never met them. I wrote a few letters but they never replied. Chris brought me messages, of course."

"Of course," Forman said, and Mike looked at him, his brows raised in a question.

"Do you have their address?"

Jane shook her head. "No, Chris always took my letters with him— Oh, they have to be told too! The poor things. And they relied on him for everything. At least I can help out."

"Both the guy at the drive-it-yourself place where he hired a car in the name of Carl Lamb and the night clerk at the Regal Motel say he had a billfold bulging with nice fresh hundred-dollar bills. Enough to cope with simple emergencies." The detective's tone was dry. He got up. "We'll want to talk to you later, Mrs. Lansing. Perhaps tomorrow. You won't be spending the night alone here, will you? Mr. Toyman said his wife would be happy—that is, she would be glad to help in any way."

"That was kind, but then she is always kind. But I think I'll go with Mike."

Mike saw the exchange of glances between the policemen.

"I'm taking her to her uncle—my uncle, too—the relationship is sort of complicated, but we've both been protégés of Uncle Jim most of our lives."

Uncle Jim, he explained, was James Moss Forsyth, who lived in one of the few private houses left on Park Avenue, an old family house that had been shut in by towering buildings but which Forsyth stubbornly refused to abandon. It would, he declared, last out his time and he was used to it. He was a stockbroker; that is, he had been, but he had retired from the Exchange a couple of years earlier because he had so many interests there was never enough time for them.

Again the two policemen exchanged glances. A member of the Stock Exchange. There seemed to be a good deal of money showing in this case.

When they had taken their leave, with Forman saying genially that he would keep in touch—Mike, at least, was aware of the subtle change in his attitude—he drew Jane to her feet. "Just tell me where your suitcase is and I'll do your packing," he said briskly, "though Uncle Jim says you left enough clothes behind to take care of anything you'd need."

"Let's just—go." Jane went into the bathroom and when she came back she had removed the traces of tears. She picked up a cheap handbag, opened it to check on keys, and Mike saw the transparent coin purse, which held two dollars and twenty-eight cents. For a moment the blood surged up the back of his head and he was almost overmastered with rage. Almost. Then he switched off the lights and Jane locked the door with a curious sense of finality.

Mike, with his usual competence, got a taxi, air-conditioned too, and gave the address of the Forsyth house on Park Avenue. Jane spoke only once on the way through Central Park.

"At least," she said, "Uncle Jim won't say 'I told you so.'"

II

The houseman beamed as he admitted Jane. "Your old rooms are ready, Miss Jane—Mrs. Lansing."

"Where's my uncle?"

"In the bookroom, but he said you weren't to bother with him. Just you rest yourself and a tray will come up later with your dinner."

Jane ignored this and went swiftly along the hallway of the narrow house, which was unexpectedly deep, to the room at the back. Heavy draperies were drawn, shutting out a small garden with a fountain, benches, and a few stunted trees, and a huge glass and steel office building on Lexington Avenue, across a narrow alley.

A Gauguin, a Manet, and the portrait of a girl who resembled Jane except for the elaborate ringlets and the evening dress that left her shoulders bare, an emerald necklace glittering on the white throat, were all beautifully lighted.

James Forsyth sat in a deep armchair, a chilled martini in his hand, staring glumly into space. In the year since Jane had seen him he had aged, his hair was gray, he had put on too much weight, and his face was more lined than she remembered. The book he held was one of his cherished set of Montaigne, but he seemed to have forgotten it, lost in unpleasant thoughts.

Jane hesitated in the doorway. "Hello, Uncle Jim," she said quietly.

He got up a trifle ponderously, took one searching look at her and another at Mike. The latter nodded and his lips shaped the word "okay."

He nodded casually as though she had been away only a couple of hours. "Want to wash up or are you ready for a cocktail?"

"I never have learned to drink much," Jane said, trying to keep her voice normal, grateful for her uncle's attitude, though she had counted on it. "We—we just couldn't afford it, except wine when we were celebrating. But maybe if there's any sherry—"

"There is always sherry," Forsyth said. He rang the bell.

"I guess maybe I'll change my dress," Jane said abruptly, and neither man looked at her, aware that her control was slipping.

They listened to her going up the stairs, not swiftly as she had in the past, but stumbling a little.

Forsyth spoke then, his voice low but so shaken with rage that Mike stared at him in astonishment. "God damn his soul to eternal hellfire! He got just what he deserved. But what has he done to her? She must have lost fifteen pounds and she looks undernourished. If I'd realized—but I didn't dare turn over her money because I thought he'd get it away from her. Still, if I had known—"

"He'd have taken every penny," Mike said grimly. "In fact, if she had had the disposal of her money, she might not be here now."

"Good God!"

"And I'd bet anything you like he was simply praying that you'd come around and offer to pay him off to get rid of him. He wasn't a man to wait."

After a moment the older man said, almost plaintively, "I never could figure out why you let her go, Mike. That would have been perfect."

"For whom? I didn't let her go, Uncle Jim. I never had her. Except when I was at college we lived here like brother and sister. Jane wasn't in love with me. I didn't have a chance."

"Well, you have a chance now."

"Good Lord, the girl is heartbroken and farther away from me now than she has ever been. It will be a long time before she is ready to take an interest in another man."

"But with you right here in the house—" Forsyth broke off as Mike shook his head emphatically.

"The police haven't sorted things out yet," he said. "There are other people involved, a plethora of motives, another so-called wife, a woman who was spending the night at the motel when he was killed and who has disappeared, an older woman whom he attempted to blackmail, and presumably men who took an interest in the women, and now—there's me. The men from Homicide arrived just as I was holding Jane in my arms, trying to comfort her. It gave them ideas. For her sake, I'm moving out of here tonight. I'll put up temporarily at the University Club. It's a hundred to one shot that they'll be checking on my alibi for last night."

"Let them try, boy. Let them try. I'll testify that you were here all night, under my own eyes. We played chess until four o'clock."

Mike grinned at him affectionately. "You old devil! You haven't the slightest idea where I was last night. And don't underestimate the police. No, I have a better idea. If you can't beat them, join them. I'm going to suggest getting a leave of absence from the *Chronicle* and working with the police to solve the murder."

"Leave of absence!" Forsyth snorted. "Anyone would think you were Foreign Editor of the *Times* instead of a legman for the *Chronicle.*"

Mike shrugged impatiently. "After all, I don't need the job and this thing has to be done."

"You wouldn't know where to look."

"At least," Mike pointed out, "I'd know where not to look."

5

TOYMAN LOOKED quickly at his wife as he came into the small house in South Orange, which they had occupied since their marriage a quarter of a century before. At forty-five she had worn well, he thought; a little overweight and some weird ideas about food, but on the whole those had been good years. He could always compensate for the unimaginative food at home by restaurant lunches, and she had been a help to him. A great help. She had come up with the idea of Tricks for Tiny Tots and she had conceived some of their cutest and best-selling items. Yes, Marge had been all he had hoped for.

Usually she tried to look her best when he came home at night, a nice dress and her face made up and wearing that Chanel Number Five she liked so much. But tonight she wore a housedress he hadn't seen for a long time and she was busy shelling peas while she watched the television screen.

She removed her glasses to wipe her eyes and she blew her reddened and swollen nose.

"You've seen it on television?" he asked.

She nodded, sniffed, went back to shelling peas. "There was a picture. He looked—he might have been asleep."

"Think of it that way, Marge."

"They say you identified him."

"Well, of course. I—have you heard from Jane?"

She shook her head.

"I told the police you'd been like a mother to that young couple. Just like a mother. I said you'd break it to Jane if it seemed best."

"No!"

"Well, apparently the police preferred to do it themselves. I guess she's taking it all right or she'd have called you."

Mrs. Toyman picked up the bowl of peas and the paper bag containing the shells and started for the kitchen. She paused as once more the picture of the blond young man, his long lashes brushing his cheeks, appeared on the screen.

"There are new developments in the case of the young man found murdered this morning at a midtown motel in New York. Registered as Carl Lamb and wife, he has been identified by the FBI as one Charles Lawrence, with a record for attempted extortion, and by a Mrs. Chester Loring, a New York model, as her husband. Michael Heald and John Toyman have both identified him as Christopher Lansing who, a year ago, married Jane Forsyth of East Hampton, New York, and Palm Beach, Florida, daughter of the late Wilbur Forsyth, Chairman of the Board of Electronics Unlimited.

"With two women claiming the dead man as their husband and a third who has disappeared without a trace, registered as his wife, the police are, so far, without a clue to the identity of the murderer. The Assistant Commissioner has announced that new developments are expected in the immediate future. Every effort is being made to find the woman who was registered as Mrs. Carl Lamb. Anyone having information—"

Marge Toyman carried the peas and shells into the kitchen, carefully poured the peas into the garbage pail and put the shells in the boiling water.

"Chris," she said in disbelief. "Not Chris."

Toyman fussily settled himself to watch his favorite program. As a man of routine it did not occur to him to change his habits but, before lighting his pipe, a matter of ritual, he sighed. "My best salesman. I'll never find another half as good. And Tricks for Tiny Tots mixed up in murder—though parents aren't apt to make the connection—and it isn't as though murder was—contaminating."

Feeling more at ease, he settled back in his favorite chair, which, over the years, had taken on the contours of his body, to watch The Wonderful World of Disney. You often picked up useful ideas from these programs.

II

Mrs. Chester Loring occupied a studio apartment in a four-story walk-up on Irving Place. The stairs had never seemed so interminable before. In fact, she had welcomed them as an excellent way of keeping her hips down and her figure in shape. But tonight she found them endless because she dreaded reaching the top, reaching the empty room.

Well, she had asked for it. She had been around, been around almost too much. That was why, when Chester became so insistent, she had decided that it was time to settle down. And he had been wonderful. Of course, not being inexperienced, and you could say that again, she had been aware that he knew a lot more about women than she did about men. So what? She was in no position to be captious. Only five months of marriage. Well, given the same choice, she'd do it again, though she had learned early on to detect when he was lying. There was always a little catch in his breath just before he was ready to tell her a whopper. She had known there was no rich aunt in Miami; she had wondered for some time what his actual job might be. Job or racket. Where she'd been a fool was in assuming that, because he seemed to be so much in love with her, his activities, whatever they were, did not involve other women.

She unlocked the door and went in to open the few small

windows—most of one wall and the ceiling formed a skylight, scorchingly hot. She turned on the electric fan, which only stirred the hot air around. She kicked off her shoes and poured a small amount of Chester's Scotch, dropped in ice, and filled the tall glass with water. She rarely took a drink. A model can't afford it. Sooner than you'd expect, it shows in the eyes, in pouches under them that are hard to conceal by makeup, even in the texture of the skin.

She sipped at the drink, made a grimace and poured it out, stripped off her clothes and took a shower. Even the cold tap was only tepid. She put on a kaftan that was almost transparent and mostly chiffon, one that Chester had enthusiastically approved, a deep pink that was becoming, though tonight that didn't matter, and came back to turn on the television. Silence made her uneasy. When there was nothing on television to enjoy, and she could watch almost anything but politics and discussion groups, she kept a radio going.

She watched as Chester's picture appeared on the screen, and listened while the new developments in the case were related. A police record? Well, that wasn't much of a surprise. There was bound to be something in Chester's brief past. But he had been identified by two men as Christopher Lansing, a toy salesman, married to another woman.

Oh, nonsense. Not Chester. He wasn't such a fool as that. Not the kind to get himself involved in some matrimonial mix-up. He didn't need that to get the girls he wanted, not with what he had.

East Hampton, Palm Beach, Chairman of the Board. Well, it could be. Pay dirt there. But if this Jane was as rich as that, why was he selling toys? Chester selling toys! That was a laugh.

Unless—the chances were that the girl's guardian or trustee would be careful not to let Chester get his hands on the purse strings. The job might be his bid to show what a sound husband he was, hard-working, worthy to get control of the girl's money. There was sense in that but it looked as though he had been outmaneuvered.

As for the dame who had vanished from the motel, there wasn't a chance the police would ever run her down. Not a chance. Mrs. Carl Lamb would never be heard of again.

There were heavy feet on the stairs and a sharp, peremptory knock. With a lithe movement she got to her feet and went to open the door. Her eyes widened when she saw the two men, recognizing what they were even before the older one held out his identification.

"Miss Barker?"

"Only professionally. I am Mrs. Chester Loring." There was defiance in her voice, her manner. After a moment's hesitation she stood away from the door. "Come in."

"Thank you." Both men took a long appreciative look at the tall, beautifully made body under its almost transparent robe. Not exactly in mourning, Detective Trimmer thought. A good looker. A stunner. Without appearing to do so, he took in the studio room with its cheap furniture, its stifling heat.

"I am Detective Trimmer and this is Sergeant Wells. We are sorry to disturb you at this time, Miss Barker—"

At this deliberate repetition of the name her eyes narrowed. "If you are trying to tell me that Chester and I weren't married," she said, her voice losing its carefully acquired gentility, "you're wrong about that, mister. We were married in Brooklyn five months ago."

"Well, the thing is," the detective eased himself into the only comfortable chair in the room, while his companion pulled out a straight chair from the card table, which served as a dining table. Both men were wary about sitting beside the girl in the froth of pink chiffon who had settled herself on the couch. With these dames you never could tell. Up to tricks, all of them. "The thing is that—uh—Chester Loring was what you might call an *alias.* According to the FBI, his real name was Charles Lawrence. And a year ago, under the name of Christopher Lansing, he married a Miss Jane Forsyth."

She took her time. "You've checked that out?"

"Oh, yes, there's no question about the marriage."

The girl was silent and the two men waited, leaving the next move up to her. She surprised them. "What is she like?"

"You mean—the other wife?"

"Yes. I take it she couldn't have been much if he was looking for a replacement at the end of seven months."

"I haven't seen her myself. My colleague reports that she is the niece of a stockbroker who retired from the Exchange a short time ago."

Beverly Barker, née Gladys Towel, raised well-marked eyebrows. "The television is way ahead of you. She's high society and gold-lined. After all, you can see Chester's point. He had what it takes and she had what he wanted. Money. But I guess she couldn't get her hands on what she had. Otherwise, believe me, he would have got it."

The two men exchanged glances. "How much," the older man asked, "do you know about your—about this guy Lawrence?"

"Is that his real name?" She shrugged. "I didn't know about another wife. I didn't know what his job really was." She added with a touch of defiance, "I didn't care what it was. I just went overboard for him." She sketched a gesture indicating the shabby room. "You can see he was no good as a provider. Hell, I can earn fifty dollars an hour as a top model, but I didn't make a point of it. It doesn't pay to hurt a man's self-esteem. I'd have put up with anything—except sharing him." And unexpectedly tears rolled down her cheeks, making the mascara streak.

The two men watched impassively. Taking one thing with another, it could be a good act. Heartbreak in pink chiffon? Maybe. Maybe not.

She sat up, dabbing at her eyes. "Oh, get out! Get the hell out and let me alone."

"Sorry, Miss Barker, but a guy has been murdered and the department wants to know why—and who."

"I can't help you."

"Where were you between, say, one and four this morning?"

"Between—" The pause seemed endless. "Is that when—?" She stood up with a lovely movement and again it was an effort to keep their eyes on her face rather than on the body gleaming under the chiffon. "But you can't think—"

"Where were you, Miss Barker?"

"I was right here."

"Can you prove that?"

"How could I?" And then her jaw dropped. "Look, I know it sounds bad but my agent was here until after four. We were going over plans for a big fashion show geared for winter cruises and that sort of thing. Planning the outfits, the kind of setting, the music to go with it, the people to get special invitations; a real champagne and caviar deal with a four-star guest list of customers."

"Your agent's name?"

"Look," she held out a hand in appeal, the nails painted gold to match her toenails, "this guy is married. The work we were doing was strictly legitimate, all business, but he's got a wife who is jealous as sin. She'd never believe it. And we couldn't work it in during the day because I've had a heavy schedule for weeks, though this is usually a slack season. Modeling winter furs in this heat is no picnic."

"His name?" the detective said patiently. "We won't make it public if we can avoid it. We aren't interested in what you were doing if you weren't at that motel."

"Find out for yourself," she said sullenly. "Get him dragged into a murder and scandal and I'll be out on my ear. His wife would divorce him, and he has a couple of kids he's devoted to."

"Okay, Miss Barker, we'll do that. And, of course, we'll keep in touch."

"I bet you will!"

"And don't leave town without notifying me, will you?"

She banged the door behind them, nearly catching the heel of one of the men. She poured a stiff drink, added little water, and swallowed it in long, thirsty gulps. She slammed the glass down on the counter beside the sink.

"I might have known. God, I might have known!"

III

James Forsyth received the two policemen in a formal and rather characterless drawing room on the front of the Park Avenue house. His real living was done in the bookroom at the back.

One of those light-moving heavy men, Detective Trimmer thought. Not a man to throw his weight around. He was too sure of himself for that, but one who was fully aware of the power he represented.

When they had introduced themselves, he shook hands briskly, a short firm handshake, and waved them to chairs.

"May I offer you a drink?"

Trimmer shook his head. "Not when we are on duty, but thank you."

"I take it you've come about this deplorable affair of my niece's husband."

Deplorable. Well, that was one word for it. No heartbreak here.

"We are sorry to have to disturb your niece at a trying time like this—"

"There's no question of disturbing her," Forsyth said blandly. "Her physician has been here and given her something to guarantee a long night's sleep."

"I'm not surprised," the detective replied with equal blandness, and the two men examined each other, duelists measuring their swords. "Perhaps you can tell me something about the man who was murdered last night."

Forsyth did not give the impression of measuring his words. He answered readily. "Actually I know practically nothing about the man. I don't even know how and where Jane encountered him. He was supposed, I understand, to be a traveling salesman for children's toys."

"That seems to be fairly well established."

"So far as I know, he came out of nowhere. Good-looking. Plausible. But, for my money, he was as phony as they come. Weak mouth. Eyes that either wouldn't look at you directly or else looked so honest and candid you'd think he was as innocent as a three-year-old."

"I take it you didn't approve of the marriage."

"I didn't approve, but I went the wrong way about it. I should have known better, with a high-spirited girl like Jane, than to run him down. But she went overboard for him and wouldn't listen to reason."

The detective grinned sympathetically. "Well, reason doesn't have a lot to do with these things, does it?"

"I suppose not. Anyhow, I told her that I absolutely refused to turn over the money she had coming from her father's estate until her husband could prove to my satisfaction that he was responsible. I wasn't going to have a ladykiller strip her of her inheritance."

"I take it that you never heard of a second marriage or of

the woman who registered as Mrs. Carl Lamb."

"Yes, you can take that." Forsyth's voice was grim. "Any lever that would have got my poor girl away from him and shattered that infatuation I'd have used without a moment's hesitation. Living in squalor, Mike tells me."

"Mike?"

"Michael Heald. Not actually related to me but like a son. He is the son of my sister's husband by an earlier marriage. I brought up the two kids, Jane and Mike. I always hoped they'd make a match of it." Instantly he was aware that he had been indiscreet.

The detective apparently studied his notes and then said in a tone of discovery, "Oh, he must be the young man who visited the morgue before news of the murder got out. He took on the task of breaking it to his—uh, to your niece."

"That's right."

"How well did he know this—I don't know what to call him. I suppose the legal name was Lawrence."

"Mike met him casually a few times. Dropped out of the picture when Jane married the fellow." Again Forsyth was aware that he had been indiscreet.

"I'd like to talk to him if he's around."

"He doesn't live here. You'll find him at the University Club."

"I suppose," Trimmer glanced at his partner, started to rise, sat down again, "you can account for your whereabouts last night. Just routine, of course."

"Of course." Forsyth considered. "I had dinner at the Algonquin with a young protégé of mine, Isaac Webber, a talented pianist who is preparing for his début. Afterwards we went to Town Hall to hear a fellow student going through the same ordeal. Not good. Not bad. Chose too ambitious a program and one not suited to his abilities. Should have stuck to something like Scarlatti and—but this isn't what you want."

He was very much at ease, very much the wealthy patron of the arts, discussing matters somewhat over the head of his listeners. Nice technique, the detective thought appreciatively. He hoped he'd never have to be involved in a clash with this man.

"We stopped for a drink somewhere. Then I walked home. Lovely evening. Read for a while. Turned in about midnight." Forsyth smiled slightly. "Not much of an alibi, is it?"

"I didn't really expect one," said the detective, returning the smile. For a moment the eyes of the two men met in amused understanding, and then they sheathed their swords.

The detective said, "We'll look up Mr. Heald. And tomorrow, of course, after she has had the rest she needs, we'll talk to Mrs.—that is, to Miss Forsyth."

Forsyth opened the door for them. Then he said unexpectedly, but with urgency in his tone, "Go easy on her, man. She's just a kid and she's had an emotional shock. This has been tough on her, tougher than you can imagine."

"Well," Trimmer commented before stepping out onto Park Avenue, "you might say it's been tough on Lawrence too, or whatever his name was. Only he can't make any defense."

The two men got into the waiting police car. From the doorway Forsyth watched it move away from the curb, into traffic.

I muffed that one, he thought. Muffed it badly. I hope to God that Mike can do better. For a moment he toyed with the idea of calling him, warning him. But the police might check on any calls. Better leave it to Mike's ingenuity.

6

IT WAS midmorning when Jane opened drugged eyes and looked in perplexity around her old familiar room. At first she thought she must still be dreaming. Then she remembered. Mike had brought her here the night before. Uncle Jim had sent for Dr. Wilkins, who had looked after her from the time she was ten years old, and he, in spite of her protests, had jabbed a hypodermic into her arm.

She hadn't wanted to sleep. There were too many unanswered questions. There were things she had to know. But though she had fought to keep awake, she had slept and, as far as she was aware, slept for—she looked at her bedside clock—it was nearly ten.

She sat up so abruptly that her head swam. For a moment she rested, her legs hanging over the side of the bed, holding on until her vision cleared. The doctor had really knocked her out.

In a wave the thought came to her: Chris is dead. Chris had been murdered. He was never really Chris at all. He was a man with a criminal record, a man with another wife, a man who had been with a third woman when he was killed, a woman who had probably killed him and then disappeared.

Chris with his gaiety, his charm, his tenderness, his passion. Chris. She rolled over on the bed but she did not cry. After a long time she got slowly to her feet and made her way waveringly into her small bathroom.

It was as though she had never left it; spotless and shining, thick soft towels, a new bar of scented soap in its wrapper, a new toothbrush and toothpaste, bath oil and eau de cologne in the cabinet. And, hanging on the back of the door, her terry-cloth bathrobe.

When she had bathed, she went back to her bedroom and dressed, choosing from a well-filled wardrobe and drawers stacked with filmy underwear.

Dressing exhausted her and she sat at the dressing table, knees shaking, while she brushed her hair and studied her face with the deep shadows under her eyes.

She rang for her breakfast tray and when the houseman set it down in her little sitting room, she managed a smile at his anxious expression.

"Good morning, Johnson. Thank you."

There was a note on the tray and she tore it open:

> Welcome home, my dear! Take it easy today. Johnson has his instructions to admit no one and to put through no telephone calls. You are to rest and worry about nothing. I have an appointment with Ralph Cummins but I should be back for lunch. Keep your chin up. Uncle Jim.

Ralph Cummins. That wasn't Uncle Jim's lawyer. This was a well-known criminal lawyer. But why? She poured coffee and crumpled a piece of toast and pushed the rest of the food away. Then she rang for Johnson, who collected the tray with a look of distress when he saw that she had eaten nothing.

"Where is Mr. Heald?" she asked. "Oh, I suppose he has gone down to the *Chronicle.*"

"Mr. Heald moved to the University Club last night. He'll

be staying there until—for a while, I guess." He did not meet her eyes.

"But—" She sat lost in thought and after a moment the houseman went out, carrying the tray. Jane looked round the pretty sitting room, which was part of the suite Uncle Jim had given her ten years earlier.

She picked up the little white telephone, put it down again, searched the telephone directory, and dialed.

Mr. Heald had taken up residence the night before, the desk clerk at the University Club said, but he did not answer his telephone. Would she care to have him paged or would she leave a message?

"No," Jane said slowly. "No message."

She went down to her uncle's bookroom, but the morning paper had already been taken away and Johnson, when she inquired, said regretfully that he had burned it in the incinerator along with the trash, as Mr. Forsyth had finished with it. So he had had his orders about that too.

She toiled up the stairs for her handbag, remembered that she was almost penniless and saw, when she opened it, that a twenty, a couple of tens, several fives, and a number of one-dollar bills had been added. Uncle Jim thought of everything. For a moment she was resentful that he had learned just how poor she had been, but somehow it no longer mattered.

This time she went down the stairs quietly, almost furtively. She heard the houseman speaking on a phone in the kitchen, placed there for the benefit of the servants and for convenience in ordering. He was saying, "I'm sorry. Miss Forsyth is taking no messages."

Miss Forsyth! The pieces were beginning to fit together. Uncle Jim was keeping her under wraps. Mike had been moved out of the house. Uncle Jim was consulting a criminal lawyer. Did that mean that the police were looking for

Chris's murderer in this house: Uncle Jim, Mike, herself?

Uncle Jim? He had opposed the marriage, done all he could to prevent it, withheld her money because he thought Chris was dishonest and that his chief interest in her was her potential wealth. But Uncle Jim wouldn't kill.

Mike? Was it Mike whom Uncle Jim was protecting, for whom he was consulting Ralph Cummins? Mike whom he had sent away from the house to forestall any speculation about the relationship between them, any suggestion that Mike had been jealous of Chris, jealous to such an extent that he would kill him? But Mike had felt only a brotherly interest in her. He wouldn't—he couldn't—and yet he had just happened to visit the morgue before the announcement of Chris's murder was made public. He had not notified the police or his newspaper of his identification of the body. Instead he had come to her.

Mike? He had no motive, she told herself fiercely. No motive. And she brushed aside her memory of his terrible rages. They had diminished as he grew older and gained self-confidence and self-control. But she had to know the truth, however sure she felt in her heart. Anything was preferable to being in doubt.

She started to open the front door, heard the murmur, and then carefully pulled it open the slightest crack. There were half a dozen men and a couple of girls waiting, several of the men with cameras. She closed the door, ran down to the basement, and out into the small garden behind the house, hoping neither Johnson nor his wife nor the maid would be glancing in that direction.

The small grass plot was already brown with summer heat and the flowers were wilting. Even the water in the fountain seemed to have little coolness as its spray struck her face. She crossed the narrow alley and entered the basement of the big glass and steel office building on Lexington, took a service elevator to the first floor and hurried out through the lobby. At the nearest drugstore she bought a scarf, which she wrapped around her head like a turban, and put on dark glasses. She hailed a taxi, thankfully one that was air-conditioned. She'd go to the *Chronicle*. Mike would help her. Mike always had been ready to help her, even as a boy when he had tormented her unmercifully. But obviously there was to be as little association as possible between them and she was oddly desolate. She had always depended on Mike.

Well, she wasn't a kid any more, not a youngster running to ask, "What shall I do now?" She had been a married woman for a year. She was able to stand on her own feet, take her destiny in her own hands.

The cabbie raised his voice in irritation. "Where to, lady? Or do you just want to ride around and cool off?"

"The New York Times," she decided quickly.

After asking questions, she was finally settled at a desk with a copy of the morning paper spread out in front of her. It was worse than she had expected. The reporters' homework having brought to light the fact that the dead man's wife was the niece of James Forsyth, plus the existence of a second wife and the disappearance of a woman who had gone to the motel with Chris—Chester—Carl—Charles—whatever his real name had been—had put the story on the front page.

Pictures on page five made Jane wince. There was one of her, a snapshot which Chris had taken and enlarged and which had stood in a cheap frame on the table in their basement apartment. That meant, didn't it, that some enterprising reporter had bribed the superintendent and got into the place? It seemed intolerable that the room which had provided the framework of that year of married life should be invaded, its corners pried into, its few belongings pawed over.

Then her eyes fell on the picture of Chris, looking as though he slept, looking as she had so often seen him. For a moment the pain seemed unbearable and then she thrust it away grimly. Chris had never existed. He had been only a dream, a dream turned nightmare. But someone had killed him, snuffed out all the lovely gaiety. A hint of his smile still lurked around the dead lips.

She could never rest until she learned the truth. Where had the money come from that he was said to have had in his wallet? What did the FBI know about him? Who was the woman who claimed to be his wife of five months? Who was the mysterious Mrs. Carl Lamb?

There was a cabinet photograph of a girl with long lovely hair and a brilliant smile, looking into the eyes of the reader. MODEL CLAIMS DEAD MAN AS HUSBAND.

For a long time Jane stared at the picture. You couldn't compete with a girl like that, she thought humbly. I always wondered what Christ saw in me when he could have had any girl.

The boy who had given her the paper looked at her curiously and Jane said, "Would it be too much trouble—may I have a pen and a piece of paper?"

"Sure, ma'am. No trouble." The boy brought them to her, looked down, saw the wide, strained, shadowed eyes. "Anything else I can do?"

She managed a smile. "Nothing, thanks," she said, trying to reassure the poor kid, and then realized that he was no younger than she, about nineteen.

Keep your mind on your job, she told herself severely, and she began to make notes. At last she leaned back, flexing her fingers. She started to tear off the written sheets from the scratch-pad the boy had given her.

"You keep it," he said. "There are plenty more." He had a moment's wild fantasy of surprising her by presenting her with a box of flowers, maybe orchids. Something to bring a smile to her eyes, but the scratch-pad was all he had to offer.

It was, Jane noticed in surprise, time for lunch and she was aware that she was hungry. At the same time she felt, unreasonably, that she had no right to have an appetite at a moment like this. She thrust on the dark glasses and went to Times Square and the nearest cafeteria, where she would be unknown. Following other people, she picked up a tray, silverware, and started down the line, choosing a chicken salad, iced coffee, and a roll and butter. She sat at a white-topped table with two other girls, apparently from nearby offices, who chattered without noticing her. She was halfway through her lunch, deep in thought, when she became aware that they were talking about Chris's murder.

"Dreamy-looking guy, wasn't he? What a waste of good material," one of the girls said. "But two wives and a spare. I ask you. I'd prefer less charm and more reliability."

"Who do you think did it?" the other girl asked. "Some weapon with a sharp point, it said on television."

"Oh, there's no mystery! It's the woman who disappeared from the motel."

"But a blow on the head?" The girl was firm about that. "A knife, maybe, or poison, but not a blow on the head. Some man behind this. Gosh, the woods must be filled with guys who had it in for him. That model, for instance. I'll bet she had a lot of boyfriends who'd be ready to tear him apart. And this Jane what's her name? Valuable property to someone. If anyone knew she was being given the runaround—well, I ask you! She looks like the kind who needs to be taken care of. Sort of cute but helpless, if you know what I mean."

"That kind always gets taken care of. Save your sympathy. Let's leave it to the police. They know their job. Anyhow I've got to hurry. I want to buy some hand lotion and skin cream before I get back to work. In this heat by five o'clock I just don't have enough energy to shop for anything but dinner."

The cashier obligingly gave Jane a dollar's worth of change and she shut herself in a telephone booth after looking up numbers. The booth was stifling and someone had been smoking in it, but she kept the door closed. She did not want her conversation overheard.

The FBI was pleasant and courteous but not forthcoming. She tried the police next, went patiently from department to department until she reached Detective Forman, the only one whose name she knew.

He was unexpectedly cooperative. "Why, sure, Miss Forsyth. Glad to help. Tell you what. Why don't you come to the precinct and we'll have a talk . . . No trouble at all. Matter of fact, I've tried to reach you at Mr. Forsyth's house but I was told you weren't taking calls and when I went there your butler, or whatever he is, said you weren't home and he was all upset about it. Didn't see you leave. And last night, I understand, your doctor made sure that you had a good rest. And Mr. Heald moved out of the house just when you moved in. University Club. Got a room there last night."

"They mean well, you know," Jane said apologetically. "It's just that they are fond of me and don't realize I've grown up."

"Of course not." Detective Forman's voice was gentle. The kid was like a one-day chick. He set down the telephone. Or was she?

II

Jane looked around her with interest as she entered the police precinct. A man coming through the doorway at the rear stopped short. "Jane! What on earth are you doing here? Have the police sent for you too?"

"Mike!" She stretched out eager hands, let them drop as she saw a policeman looking at her, did a double take.

"You mean they sent for you?"

"Just routine, you know," he said carelessly.

"What did they want?"

"Drop it, baby, and let's get out of here."

"I have an appointment with Detective Forman."

"I'm coming with you. Oh," he stood frowning down at her. "No, I'll call Uncle Jim and have him get hold of his tame lawyer."

"You'll do nothing of the kind," she said firmly. "But I do wish you'd call the house and say I had to go out on business and I'll be back later. Uncle Jim might worry."

"You're damned right he'll worry. I'll wait here for you."

She touched his arm then, pleading. "Please, Mike!"

"All right," he conceded reluctantly. He grinned at her. "All right, baby. Have it your way."

She watched him go out of the station and then followed the policeman into a small room that held three desks with just room at each for two chairs. Only one desk was occupied.

"Well, look who's here!" Detective Forman pushed back his chair and edged his way around the desk to shake hands with her. "Nice to see you, Miss Forsyth. Sit in that chair and you'll feel the fan." He reached tentatively for the jacket hanging over the back of his chair and she shook her head.

"Oh, please don't. It's too hot. And I won't take up much of your time. Only—" She sat for a moment, hands clasped on her lap, her eyes on them, considering. Then she looked up. "You see, I've got to know."

"You want to know who killed your—this guy? Well, so do we."

"That, of course, but—well, I don't seem to have known anything. His criminal record. The other wife. The woman who was with him when he was killed and who ran away. What he was really like. No matter how bad it is, I'd rather know the truth. Right now there is quicksand under my feet and I want solid ground. No matter what."

He found himself believing her; the colorless face and the shadowed eyes aroused his pity. Her doctor might have assured her a night's sleep, but it didn't seem to have done her much good. She looked lost. And haunted.

As a rule he didn't waste much sympathy on poor little rich girls. Usually, in his experience, they were spoiled brats. But this one was—well, not defenseless. Not defenseless at all. There was determination in her chin, in the directness of her eyes. She could take it.

"We've just started, you know," he said. "There are so many damned—excuse me—ramifications. You'd be surprised to know how many men we have out asking questions, trying to get a line on the man's background. We aren't neglecting the murder angle, naturally, but murder doesn't crop up out of nothing. We're looking for a motive: jealousy, revenge, partners in crime falling out, husbands or fathers or lovers wanting to stop his activities."

"I see. It's queer, you know, to find I've been living the kind of thing you see in soap operas. Not dramatic, not romantic, not even pathetic. Just sordid, sordid and ugly." She was silent for a moment and he waited. "It's odd, you know," she said in a tone of surprise. "Before I got married, Uncle Jim said that one of two things would happen: either I'd find out what Chris was and be made unhappy or I'd grow like him. A shoddy Jane. Something like that."

Forman nodded. Well, you had to hand it to her. She was taking it on the chin. Remembering the good-looking face with its hint of a mocking smile, the eyes with their fringe of heavy lashes, and recalling his wife's wistful comments when she saw it, he could understand something of the shock and pain she was enduring at this moment behind the quiet, exhausted little face. Probably it was the first time in her life that she had come up against disillusionment.

"Suppose," he said, "you begin by telling me all you know about your—about this Chris, as you called him. Where and how you met him, what friends he had, what you know about his job and his family, anything at all."

They had met at a charity ball she had attended with a small party of friends. He had come up to her and introduced himself as Christopher Lansing and they had danced. Danced again. Made a date to meet for cocktails and then, when she said she didn't care much for cocktails, they had had lunch at an odd but amusing little restaurant she had never heard of.

Keeping her under wraps, Forman said to himself. The door opened and a plainclothes detective came in, saw Forman's shake of the head and, after a quick look at Jane, withdrew, closing the door quietly behind him.

They had met for lunch several times and twice he had taken her out to dinner and dancing. Again he had chosen offbeat places. He had told her that he sold children's toys and he had to travel a lot but the work was interesting and he was the restless sort who liked being on the move. She caught her breath, and Forman waited patiently.

He had said his only family consisted of his mother and one sister. The mother was crippled with arthritis and the sister was mentally retarded. A terrible burden for him, but he took for granted that it was his job to look after them and, whenever he could, perhaps once every six weeks, he went up to Buffalo to see them.

"I just fell head over heels in love with him," Jane said, her chin high, looking straight at the detective. "Just head over heels. So when he wanted us to get married right away, I said I would. When he found out I had a bit of money, he was afraid—he said he was afraid," she corrected herself carefully. "He said it would make a differeence. He thought

Uncle Jim would say he wasn't good enough for me."

"And he was right about that," Forman said.

As Jane looked at him questioningly, he nodded. "Yes, one of our men talked to him last night. He was dead against the guy from the first. Tried to persuade you not to marry him, and protected you the best he could by holding out your money. Right?" When she made no reply, he said thoughtfully, "Yes, sir, Mr. Forsyth didn't like him at all; he didn't want any part of him."

"But Uncle Jim wouldn't—" she began quickly. Stopped.

"Wouldn't kill him to set you free? Even if he learned of his other—activities?"

"No. No. Not Uncle Jim!"

"Well, go on."

"So we got married anyhow and took the little basement apartment on West Ninetieth Street where you found me yesterday. It wasn't to be for long because his boss plans to retire in another year and we had an idea, in fact we were almost certain from something that was said, that he was going to make Chris his successor. He loved him just like a son. He and Mrs. Toyman both. She couldn't have been nicer. We'd go over to New Jersey now and then for dinner —the craziest dinners," and a smile quivered on her lips. "Little dishes of nuts and raisins and things cooked with seaweed and herbs that were supposed to have magical properties, keep you young and healthy and I don't know what all.

"Always afterwards we'd go somewhere and have fish and chips or a hamburger because Chris couldn't stand the stuff. But Mrs. Toyman was a dear. She'd come to see me lots of afternoons and we'd just talk. She hasn't any children of her own and she's crazy about young people and especially little children. That's how she happened to develop the idea of Tricks for Tiny Tots. She is the one who thinks them up and makes the designs. You'd never believe she could think up such things. Her house is just wild with models of some of their best sellers all around the place.

"And now she's branched out into Tricks for Teenagers and the business is really booming. A magic set with all sorts of gadgets, even sawing the lady in half. And a James Bond set with the goofiest things. Instead of just Christmas and birthday sales, shops are giving Chris huge orders every month, and the annual toy show in New York is breaking records. Mr. Toyman expects to take on more workmen just to keep up with the orders."

The enthusiasm faded. "I guess the Toymans will mind more than anyone else, especially Mrs. Toyman. Mr. Toyman is so fidgety and set in his ways that nothing can change him much. But then he's awfully old. But he'll never," she added, pride in her voice, "find anyone to replace Chris."

And that, it appeared, was all that Jane had to tell. She answered all the detective's questions painstakingly but nothing new emerged. Then she said, "I've answered a lot of questions. May I ask some?"

"Of course, little lady."

She winced at the little lady, thinking how Chris would laugh at that. "I wish you would tell me three things: First, what does the FBI know about him? Second, what do you know about Chris's—second wife? Third, do you have any clue to the woman who registered with him at the motel?"

The FBI, he told her, had come up with the man's real identity. He was Charles Lawrence who had been arrested two years earlier for attempted extortion of a Mrs. Harrison Fitch. Mrs. Fitch, a wealthy woman of fifty, had withdrawn her complaint and the case had never come to trial.

"Fitch," Jane said, her brow furrowed. "I'm pretty sure Uncle Jim used to know a Harrison Fitch. I think he was on the Exchange with him or something. But that was a long time ago."

To Forman's relief she did not ask for the woman's address. He had already learned that she had an unlisted telephone number, which the FBI had given him. He did not want Jane muddying the waters and there was a never-give-up quality about her that he profoundly distrusted.

At the same moment Jane was making a mental note to look in the Social Register when she got home. There would be no problem in finding Mrs. Fitch.

"I saw the pictures of—the other one," she said wistfully. "She's terribly attractive, isn't she?"

"In a way," Forman admitted, "though I haven't seen her myself, except the picture in the paper. But you keep away from her. According to the men who interviewed her, she's one tough cookie. Attractive? Sure. But all the goods are on display, if you get what I mean." He looked at her doubtfully. She probably didn't. "Behind it there's nothing, not much in the way of brains, not the kind of girl a guy wants to marry." He broke off. That had been a dumb thing to say!

"Except," Jane pointed out with a wry smile, "that one did. You think she's tough. Do you suppose, if she was suspicious of Chris or Chester or whatever she called him, she could have followed him to the motel and—"

"Now you leave this to us. That's an order, little lady. We know our job. You give this Loring girl, Beverly Barker or whatever she calls herself professionally, a wide berth. Anyhow," as he saw the obstinate set of her lips, "she claims to have an alibi for the essential time. We're checking it out, along with a lot of other stuff."

"And the woman at the motel?"

He shrugged. "You pays your money and you takes your choice. Not a clue. Not a fingerprint. Not one of those convenient handkerchiefs with her initials or a letter with her name. Strictly professional this job was."

He silenced the jangling of the telephone. "Forman." Then he said, "Yeah . . . Yeah . . . You can't win them all." His eyes were on Jane and she was aware that the conversation concerned her in some way. "Sure it looks odd, dragging out the heavy artillery before war is declared. Keep at it."

When he set down the telephone, Jane got to her feet. "Thank you very much for giving me so much time and being so helpful." She held out her hand, which was engulfed in his.

"That's what we are here for," he assured her.

She paused at the door, as though the thought had just occurred to her. "Oh, by the way," she said with elaborate carelessness, "I ran into my cousin Mike as I was coming in. What on earth was he doing here?"

"Like you, he was asking questions." Forman added, "And answering a few."

7

ON THE STREET Jane hunted for a bit of shade from the blistering heat and stood in a doorway while she consulted her notes. She looked for a taxi and finally got on a bus, fumbling for change, which she dropped with a clink, and held onto the seats as she made her way back toward the center exit.

Apparently it was the wrong bus, for she had to walk a number of blocks and make a detour around Gramercy Park, baking in the sun, its famous old clubs sleeping the hot afternoon away, until she reached Irving Place, and passed the old Washington Irving house, looking for numbers. The one she sought was in a shabby walk-up, with a row of mailboxes in a dark hallway. The front door stood open. She looked at the names under the mailboxes, saw one with two names: Beverly Barker, Chester Loring, and the word Studio. Clear at the top then.

She went slowly up the uncarpeted stairs, passed a sign, "Home Dressmaking and Alterations. Walk in," and through the open door saw an elderly woman who looked up hopefully from a sewing machine and then, as Jane did not stop, bent over her work again. On the third floor the sound of an acrimonious discussion came from behind a closed door. There was only one door on the fourth floor. Jane waited for her heart to slow down. The stairs and her own nervousness had left her slightly breathless.

Her knock was answered by a quick "Who's there?"

Jane hesitated. "Miss Barker? I'm—I'm Chris's wife."

The door was flung open. The girl was very tall and somehow not as alluring as she had seemed in the picture but that, of course, had been posed. She wore tight jeans cut off jaggedly at the knees, and a bra. Her feet were bare and the gold polish was peeling off her toenails. Her face was puffy and the long blond hair was disheveled. She pushed it back absently as she stared at the smaller girl. Dislike—curiosity—then a rather cruel amusement.

"My God, he was really robbing the cradle! Come in, kid. Sit down if you can find a place." She looked doubtfully at the disorderly room, the unmade bed, the clothes strewn on chairs, the card table with the cup of coffee, a fried egg chilling on a plate, a piece of half-eaten toast.

"Oh, I've interrupted your lunch."

"Brunch. I wasn't hungry. I didn't sleep much and when I did, I had these dreams—God! Did you see Chester at the morgue?"

Chester? "No, my cousin and his boss, Mr. Henry Toyman, identified him."

"So he really had a boss! What was his racket, did you ever find out?"

"He was a traveling salesman for children's toys," Jane said a trifle stiffly.

Beverly Barker let out an unexpected crackle of laughter. "Chester selling children's toys!"

"He was very good at it, the best salesman they ever had, and we think—thought—Mr. Toyman planned to turn the business over to him in another year."

"Chester told you that? Didn't you ever get onto when he was lying?"

Jane made no answer.

"So you actually met his boss." Beverly was surprised.

"And his wife. We had dinner there at his house in New Jersey and she used to come over to see me and give me ideas about housekeeping and shopping and all that. She was like a mother to us."

"With your money I don't see why you needed to know about housekeeping."

"I haven't any money. Uncle Jim thought," Jane hesitated, "it was better for a young couple to try to make it on their own."

"Yeah? You mean he didn't trust Chester an inch. I guess Chester wouldn't be in his class. He wouldn't be able to put it over on a big capitalist. But, God, he was one lovable man!" The model blinked back tears. "Or didn't you think so?"

"We were—I was in love," Jane said. "I never guessed—all that time—he had—there was—another one."

"Neither did I," Beverly admitted. "And let me tell you, sister, it's just as well for you I didn't. Playing around? Okay, you've got to give a guy—and a gal, for that matter—some rope. But another wife—the hell with that!"

She saw that Jane was looking around her as though trying to imagine Chester—or what did she call him?—in these surroundings.

"Why did you come here?"

"I was curious," Jane admitted. "I wondered what kind of woman Chris would turn to after just seven months, when he still seemed to be so much in love with me. I wondered what you had to give him that I didn't have."

"Well?" There was a mocking challenge in the other girl's face.

"Oh, yes, I see now." Jane's manner was so courteous that it was a full minute before angry color rose in Beverly's cheeks.

"You have the hell of a nerve coming here! If you've satisfied your curiosity, do me a favor and get out."

"Well, not quite satisfied it." Jane's voice was still courteous. "I was wondering, of course, if you're so jealous of competition, where you were when Chris was killed."

"The police are satisfied."

"Are they? Somehow I didn't get that impression. They won't rest—and I won't rest—until the truth comes out."

On that note Jane went out and closed the door quietly behind her. As she started down the stairs, there was a crash as Beverly hurled some metal object against the door.

II

Back at Gramercy Park, Jane picked up a cab, which had just unloaded passengers at The Players, and gave the address of the Park Avenue house.

When Johnson let her in, an expression of relief on his face, she touched her lips with a finger and went quietly upstairs. In her sitting room she searched the bookshelves for the Social Register. Mrs. Harrison Fitch lived, as might be expected, in the Turtle Bay section.

Jane paused long enough to change to a soft green sleeveless dress that made her look as cool as crisp lettuce, fastened a string of pearls around her neck and matching pearl studs in her ears from the jewelbox she had left behind when she married. Married?

Johnson was waiting in the hall when she went down, this time determined not to let her leave the house.

"Tell Mr. Forsyth that I've gone to call on a friend and that I'll be back within an hour," she said.

"He wanted to see you particular as soon as you came in."

"Later," she said firmly and went out. The doorman under the canopy of the huge apartment building next door whistled for a taxi and deftly palmed her tip. The Turtle Bay house was small, perhaps four stories in height, and narrow, with an unexpected quality of gaiety. Four steps led up to a door painted a bright green and there were green shutters against the red-brick walls. On either side of the steps there were bright-colored flowers in heavy tubs that could not be knocked over by wind. A welcoming sort of house.

There was an odd expression on the maid's face when she came back to report that Mrs. Fitch would receive her but she had only a few minutes to spare as she had an appointment within a half hour.

She was sitting in a brightly lighted room at the back of the house, which looked down on a small, well-kept garden. The furniture was cretonne-covered and as gay as the exterior. Air-conditioning made the room pleasant, as did the tall vases of roses whose fragrance scented the air.

Mrs. Fitch was in her middle fifties, somewhat overweight, her hair in the process of returning to its natural gray from a dark dye. She wore little makeup and no jewelry except for wedding and engagement rings, but the simple dress that made the best of her figure must have cost at least two hundred and fifty dollars, as far as Jane could estimate.

She was sitting near the window, working at a piece of needlepoint and listening to a recording of Badura-Skoda playing Schubert. She turned to smile at Jane, but her eyes were strained as she looked searchingly at the girl. Then she switched off the record player, put down the needlepoint, and came to hold out a plump but beautifully cared-for hand with lovely oval nails.

"Sit down, my dear. No, not that chair. You're such a tiny thing you'd be lost. Try this one. We are really old friends, you know. My husband and Jim Forsyth were closely associated for years and years and I know him well. And this past year," there was a tiny pause, "since your marriage, I've persuaded him to dine here occasionally. He was lonely without you."

While Jane was seating herself, Mrs. Fitch went on, chattering nervously. "And that attractive cousin of yours! I never see hide nor hair of him. Of course," again the pause, "young men have no time for—old women."

Up to this point Jane had felt shock, agonizing loss, grief, disillusionment. Her meeting with Beverly, Chris's second wife, if either of them had been legally married, had increased her disillusionment. She could not be jealous of such blatant vulgarity, aware only of a kind of weary disgust. And yet the girl had been valued by Chris, loved by him, or whatever passed for love with him. It was with Beverly that he had spent so much time when she had assumed he was on the road.

But Mrs. Harrison Fitch, creeping up on old age, beginning to accept old age as though something had finished for her, was a different matter. Perhaps the woman had been a fool. Undoubtedly she had been a fool. But Chris could be so charming, so convincing. Jane was angry with him now. Using this gullible woman who, for all her apparent sophistication, her woman-of-the-world aura, gave an odd impression of innocence had been a piece of calculated brutality, of cruel cynicism.

Why, he was only a gigolo, she thought, living on woman. Was that what he had expected of her—that Uncle Jim would relent, turn over her money or perhaps buy him off?

She did not want to know what had happened between Chris and Mrs. Fitch. What she knew was enough; he had hurt her, not only in her dignity, her faith in herself, her self-respect, but he had attempted blackmail. He had made her see that he expected her to pay for the time he had spent with her. And through newspapers and television she had learned of the real background of the man, of his marriages, one of them to the niece of an old friend, of his murder. And now she was probably wondering, in anguish, whether Jane knew of her former association with Chris.

Jane was surprised to find that at last she was free of Chris, free of pain, ready to face the future with fresh hope, and she owed it to Mrs. Fitch.

So she returned the anxious, searching look with a warm smile. "I guess," she said naïvely, "there's no tactful way of going at this, but I just want to tell you that I am ashamed of Chris and what he did to you."

The two women looked at each other, the bleak truth between them.

"How did you know?" Mrs. Fitch said at last.

"The FBI had his fingerprints and identified him as Charles Lawrence. They said he had a record of arrest but no conviction. I found out the truth from the police. But," she added hastily, "they won't bother you. At least I don't think they will. Except, of course, they are going to do their best to learn who the woman at the motel was and to get alibis from everyone who was ever associated with Chris. That's only fair because there are so many who might be unjustly suspected."

"Do I understand that you are helping the police?"

"There isn't much I could do, but, of course, I am in a better position than they are to check on some things. They didn't give me your address, you know. I found it in the Social Register. I didn't like to ask Uncle Jim. And I think, Mrs. Fitch, it would be a good idea for you to make sure you have some sort of alibi that can't be broken. Like dinner at the White House or something."

"Do you feel that you are wise to interfere?" Mrs. Fitch asked coldly.

"Well, I had to know. Know who and what Chris really

was. And now that I know, I am free of him. I've just seen the woman he married seven months after he married me. She's cheap and vulgar and possessive. I keep wondering if she followed him to the motel night before last and killed him and then drove the other woman away or found her killing him—"

Jane broke off as she became aware of the other woman's raddled face. "I'm sorry. I'm so sorry. I had no right to come, but I wanted to know and I had to talk to someone who could understand, could share—" She flung out both hands. "I keep saying the wrong thing."

For a long time they looked at each other, the older woman and the girl, unspoken thoughts between them. Then, with a sudden gesture of mute apology, Jane got up and went out of the room.

When the front door had closed behind her, Mrs. Fitch rang the bell. "I have a terrific headache. I'm going to lie down and I don't want to be disturbed until I ring."

In her room she paced up and down. The girl had the insolence to come to her, armed with the knowledge that had, she hoped, been buried in the police files. She said an alibi would be required of her. She said there were things she could do better than the police. That meant, didn't it, the letters she had been mad enough to write, letters Charles had used for his attempted extortion. But it was not of Charles she was thinking, but of Charles's young wife who probably had the letters in her possession. Or could it be the other wife?

III

Jane went down the stairs with their bright borders of flowers. But the police didn't say they weren't going to bother Mrs. Fitch, she thought. I did all the talking. She just listened. She must have thought I was awful, barging in on her like that. How badly Chris must have hurt her!

But who would think, Jane wondered with the arrogance of nineteen, who would ever believe a woman that old could fall in love and let a young man like Chris make a fool of her? I suppose there's more feeling than I realized under that controlled manner. Perhaps a lot more feeling. And Chris, with his beguiling ways, had aroused a storm of emotion in a woman old enough to be his mother. Jane turned away from the thought. It was indecent.

She walked blindly. I should have left it to the police. I should never have gone there, never let her know that I know.

She turned left, walking toward Park Avenue. So far only women had surfaced in Chris's background. Where had that bulging billfold of new hundred-dollar bills come from? Blackmail that paid off? Beverly Barker would never have paid a cent, that was for sure. But Mrs. Fitch—if he had her again in his toils—would she? Would she pay up and then—?

Oh, not Mrs. Fitch, Jane thought. She just isn't capable of violence. Anyone who likes to surround herself with such pretty flowers, such gay settings—but it wasn't altogether convincing. She didn't think her reasoning would convince Detective Forman, but then Detective Forman didn't have to know about Mrs. Fitch's pain and humiliation, the hair returning to its natural gray because she no longer strove to be young, no longer had a reason to be young.

Jane turned onto Park Avenue with its lanes of moving cars, doormen whistling for taxis, the beautiful esplanade. It was a lovely street, she thought, with a building blocking the south end and traffic dividing around it like a stream around an island, and the dazzling light on eastern windows from the afternoon sun. She walked more quickly. It was good to be home, back in the world to which she belonged. In a little while, she thought, I'll forget I ever left it.

8

"COME ALONG," Forsyth said over the telephone. "Jane isn't here. . . . I don't know. She's gone off on her own hook. . . . Police precinct! . . . Well, you might as well come have a drink and dinner, at least. I probably made a mistake in shipping you off to the University Club. That will cause more speculation than if I had let you stay. By the time the police got through with Johnson and his wife and the maid last night they were thinking plenty. You could almost see the wheels go round. Can't blame the servants. I fell into a couple of obvious traps when they talked to me."

He settled down with a book, but after a few moments it lay unheeded on his lap. What on earth had possessed Jane to go to the police? He had made sure that they could not reach her by telephone or at the house and then she had slipped out on her own and gone to see them. Mike had encountered her there and she had refused to let him wait for her. Well, she might have been right about that. At this point he did not know what was right or expedient. But he knew that Ralph Cummins would disapprove violently of Jane taking any steps on her own.

Time dragged until he heard Mike's voice in the hall and saw him appear in the doorway, summoning up a grin, though he looked white and drawn.

"Go take a cold shower," Forsyth directed after a look

at him, "before we try to talk."

Mike ran lightly upstairs to the rooms that had been his for so long and returned in a short time, a little color in his face from a brisk rubdown, freshly shaven, and his hair still wet from the shower. He sprawled in a deep chair facing Forsyth across the empty fireplace, and let his head drop against the back of his chair, enjoying the air-conditioning.

"Want a drink?"

"Not yet, thanks. Well?"

"Let's be orderly about this," Forsyth said. "Get things organized."

Mike grinned at him affectionately. Uncle Jim always had to get things organized before taking any steps.

"Last night, after you'd gone off to the University Club, the police came back, after having had a go at me, and tackled the servants. I think that was a tactical error on my part. You've always lived here. Your moving simply aroused unfortunate speculations. You might as well come back."

"I aroused the speculations myself," Mike said. "The first look the police had at me was when I was holding Jane in my arms. I'd just broken the news to her."

"How did it happen you were the first to identify Chris or whoever he was?" Forsyth's voice was casual but his eyes were intent.

"The *Chronicle* doesn't start men at the top. I've been there just two months and I haven't yet had the scoop of the century or made headlines on the front page. I'm strictly a legman. One of my less engaging duties is checking on the morgue. As luck would have it, the attendant I've seen there in the past, the one who knows me, is out with a slipped disc, and the replacement didn't know me from Adam."

"When the police called here last night they thought it odd that a newspaperman would not at once inform his editor of the man's identity, even if he withheld it from the authorities."

"Better me than the police breaking it to Jane. I couldn't just let them walk in on her, unprepared and all."

Forsyth said with his usual understatement, "You see, Mike, we seem to be facing a bit of a problem. The police naturally are looking for a motive for Chris's murder. Now they have me—"

"You!" Mike's eyes almost bulged and Forsyth laughed.

"Me. I hated the man's guts and I didn't want Jane to marry him. I held out her money, which I have a legal right to do, according to the trust. And, supposing I discovered the existence of a second wife or had him followed and knew he had gone to a certain motel with a woman, I might do my best to eliminate him. And I haven't an alibi for the time when he was killed."

Forsyth brought his plump hands together, fitting the fingertips carefully as though much depended on it. "And then there is you. You see the body in the morgue before the story hits the press and you set off at top speed to find Jane. You are discovered holding her in your arms."

When Mike made no comment, Forsyth went on. "I did a lot of thinking last night. This morning, after doing my best to keep Jane *hors de combat,* I made an appointment with Ralph Cummins."

"You really pulled out the heavy artillery," Mike said in a tone of awe. "But, Uncle Jim, was that wise? If there was speculation before—I mean—"

"I know what you mean. It sounds as though either you or I might need legal defense before too long. Well, boy, that's exactly what it does mean. We're the two obvious suspects. We love the girl and we wanted this man out of her life. Permanently."

"But if the police find out about Cummins, that will make us even more suspect, won't it?" Mike thought it over. "What did Cummins have to say?"

"He thinks it is serious. He wants to see Jane, and, if necessary, put her in a nursing home, incommunicado, as long as possible."

"He doesn't know Jane."

"And he wants to see you, explore your activities the night Chris died—" Forsyth broke off. "What's wrong about that?"

Mike tried to laugh but the effect was not convincing. "Just one of those things. You remember Mack Milford?"

"Milford? One of your Princeton friends? Here occasionally for a weekend?"

Mike nodded.

"What about him?"

"He got married yesterday. At least I suppose he did. I was one of thirteen who threw a bachelor's dinner for him the night before. Too many beaded bubbles bursting at the brim. I couldn't put that evening together again to save my life."

"It might literally come to that." Forsyth was not amused.

"Well, someone apparently poured me into a taxi and I got back home about half-past four or five in the morning. Not that I could read my watch. The taxi driver took my key and unlocked the door for me. And that, as they say, is that."

"I'll have Cummins get on it. Bound to turn up someone who remembered you at the party or the taxi driver who would know where and when he picked you up."

"Oh, the police have probably done that already. They sent for me this morning."

"My God!" Forsyth's hands gripped his chair arms and he sat upright, braced for action. "They didn't let you call a lawyer? They didn't inform you of your rights?"

"I wasn't arrested. Just questioned. I told them all I could remember about what the papers will undoubtedly call The Murder Night." Seeing his uncle's expression, Mike said bluntly, "It's one hell of an alibi; I know that as well as you do; but it's the only one I have."

"You told this to the police?"

"Sure. I also told them I had met Chris just three times before Jane married him and that I had never seen him since. I didn't even know where they lived until I called you after I'd been to the morgue. I admitted I hadn't liked the guy and, because I was fond of Jane and didn't want any bickering, I had stayed away."

"Did you find out anything helpful?"

"Apparently Chris was really working for a man named Toyman, selling children's toys. The man seems to have thought highly of him, thought he was a great salesman, and treated him like one of his own family. The police also confirmed the second marriage, five months ago, in Brooklyn, to a model named Beverly Barker, or using that as a professional name. You must have seen her picture in the morning paper."

Forsyth nodded. "He seems to have had a very catholic taste in women. Nothing about the woman at the motel?"

"Not that the police were handing out."

"A gold digger who killed him after he had given her all he had?"

Mike shook his head. "I think we can eliminate that possibility. Apparently Chris was loaded with new hundred-dollar bills. But he was the kind who took them from women, not the kind who handed them out. You should have seen Jane's basement apartment. About half the size of this room, with a few pieces of broken-down secondhand furniture she had tried to brighten up. I'd like to think the murder was the work of the second wife, but murder like that is cold-blooded, and with a woman it would probably be a hot-blooded deal."

"What's the difference?"

"This one was cool. Not a fingerprint in the place. No wallet. No hint of identification. Pockets of his clothes empty. All this took time, and a woman in a jealous rage wouldn't be able to think that way, or a woman who had killed. She'd want, above all, to get out in a hurry. Someone took his time over this one."

"None of this is going to be of much comfort to Cummins. Did the police ask anything more?"

"Oh, sure. Took my fingerprints—with my permission. Asked about my record, what I did for a living, where I lived, et cetera, et cetera. Oh, I explained that I had no reason to rob Chris. I didn't need a job to get enough to eat. I wasn't your pensioner, though God knows the debt of gratitude I owe you—"

Forsyth made an abrupt gesture. "That's enough of that nonsense. You and Jane have been like my own children."

"At least, Jane really is your niece, but I have no claim on you at all, just the son of your sister's first husband by a former marriage."

"Well," Forsyth said, cornered, "your mother was a very nice girl. And, damn it, I have a perfect right to share my house with you if I want to."

Mike grinned at him. "I'm not going to say any more about it, Uncle Jim. But what brought this up was the subject of my income. I explained that my father had left my mother fairly well off and when, after his death, she married a second wealthy guy, she turned over my own father's holdings to me, with you as trustee. I said I wasn't rich but I had a regular income of about thirty-five thousand a year and that I drew on comparatively little of it, as I live here and have no big expenses and no special taste for high living."

The two men were silent, lost in thought, and when Forsyth finally broke the silence it was to say, so casually that Mike was alerted, "One thing I thank God for, Mike. You've outgrown your old childhood tantrums. I don't suppose anyone could testify to having seen you in one of those rages in years."

He broke off as there were voices in the hall and then Jane appeared in the doorway, followed by Johnson, who seemed to be herding her along for fear she would escape.

The two men got up and Forsyth said, "Time you got back. A sweltering day and you look a bit pale. How about a gin and tonic with a dash of lime?"

"I'd rather have some iced tea, quarts of it," Jane said lightly, looking from one anxious face to the other.

Forsyth nodded. "Iced tea for—Miss Forsyth and gin and tonic for me. Yours, Mike?"

"The same."

Jane began to laugh. "All right," she said. "I'll talk."

"What made you—" Forsyth and Mike began together. Stopped at something in Jane's face. She'd been doing a lot of growing up in the past year and it would be as well to remember that fact.

"Well, when Johnson said there wasn't a morning paper in the house and that you had an appointment with Mr. Cummins who, so far as I know, is the top criminal lawyer, I decided that I had to know."

"Know what?"

"Everything," she said simply. She recounted her day, beginning with the abortive call to Mike, when she found he had left home, and then going to *The New York Times* to learn just what had happened, at least how much the police had revealed to the press. "One thing about the *Times*. They may not put it in bold headlines, but they always have complete coverage. Well, then I had some lunch—"

"It's a wonder to me you weren't mobbed," Mike said so sharply that she was surprised. It wasn't like him to be genuinely angry with her. "You've been photographed often enough."

Mike's anger made Forsyth raise an eyebrow and then smile faintly. If Jane ever came out of her infatuation for Chris, Mike would be competent to handle her and curb some of her wilder impulses.

"I went over to Lexington and bought dark glasses and a scarf to cover my hair. You wouldn't have known me yourself."

"Bet I would."

"Bet you wouldn't. Anyhow, I called the FBI to try to find out about Chris's real identity and his fingerprints and record. They wouldn't tell me anything. So then I finally found out where to reach Detective Forman, because he was the only one whose name I knew, and that's where I ran into you. What did they want with you?"

"Just a list of previous arrests, the number of terms I'd served in the Big House, and why I was not reporting to my parole officer," he said out of the corner of his mouth.

"Oh, shut up! This is serious. Anyhow," and she described her visit to Detective Forman, and what she had learned from him.

The two men exchanged glances over her head while she took the tall glass of iced tea from the tray and they reached for gin and tonic. For a moment they sipped in contented peace. Then Forsyth said, after studying Jane's innocent face suspiciously, "Okay, let's have the worst. What did you do next?"

"I went to see the other—I called on the model who married Chris, only she calls him Chester." Jane's tone was defiant.

"You shouldn't be allowed out alone," Mike said in a tone of disgust.

"If Uncle Jim had had his way," she flashed, "I wouldn't be. Having the doctor practically knock me out, saying I couldn't answer the telephone or talk to anyone. Even having the morning paper burned. I apologized to the detective," she said kindly, "and explained that you meant well."

Mike choked over his drink. "I suppose the detective just opened his heart and poured out his soul to you."

"I'll bet he told me a lot more than he told you," she retorted.

Hearing the familiar bickering exchange that put both Mike and Jane on a teen-age level, Forsyth relaxed in his chair.

"And what earth-shaking secret did he confide in your shell-like ear?" Mike asked sweetly.

"He told me the other one—Beverly—had an alibi for the night Chris was killed, only I don't think he believed it. And when she was so mean to me, practically sneering in my face, I told her so. That shook her."

"What I should do by rights," Mike said, "is to turn you over my knee and beat the tar out of you. Of all the dimwitted—"

"And then," she ignored him, turned her attention to Forsyth, after drinking thirstily, "I went to see Mrs. Harrison Fitch."

Forsyth set down his empty glass. "Hank Fitch's widow?" he said blankly. "What in hell—"

"She's the reason for Chris's record. I mean she had him arrested for blackmail or extortion—or are they the same thing?—and then at the last minute she withdrew the charge so she wouldn't have any ugly publicity, I suppose. That's why the FBI had his fingerprints and knew his real name, which is Charles Lawrence. He always used the same initials, didn't he? C.L. Probably that made it easier to remember so many names."

Something in her voice, a kind of detachment, brought the eyes of the two men together again. Mike, under cover of his broad chair arm, made a circle of thumb and forefinger. Forsyth nodded. However injudicious her day's activities had been, they had helped Jane adjust to a knowledge of the man she had loved and lost.

"I remembered you and Mr. Fitch used to be great friends, so I looked her up in the Social Register and went to see her."

Hearing Forsyth gasp, she nodded agreement. "I know, it was kind of brash, not even knowing her and all. But she was so nice—in the beginning—and said she was fond of you and felt we were old friends. Only when I saw what Chris had done to her—her pride shattered and her hair going gray again as though she didn't care, and something shattered deep down—I can't explain, but any woman would understand. I was so angry with him."

Neither man knew what to say. Johnson came in to refill the glasses and still the silence remained unbroken.

"She's nice," Jane said at last. "Awfully nice. But Chris destroyed something in her. I kept wondering, suppose Chris had come back and fooled her again. He was so devastating in some ways. So irresistible. I suppose any woman—well, I wondered about all that money he was said to be flashing around. Suppose—she'd hardly see him at her house—but suppose she went to the motel and gave him the money and —" Her voice trailed off.

"Look here, Jane," Forsyth said with unaccustomed sternness, "you can't say things like that. Slander. Hank Fitch's widow! Good God! Caesar's wife."

"But not two years ago when she had Chris arrested. I don't mean she was the only one. I don't think that model would have been willing to share him. She—when I as good as told her the police didn't believe her alibi and went out, she threw something at the door." Jane added, "A blunt instrument."

Forsyth was speechless but Mike was more resilient. "What a line," he said admiringly. "You should be writing the dialogue for Hawaii Five-O. All I'm waiting for is the big curving wave to provide the appropriate and appreciative pause."

Jane swung around to glare at him, met his mocking eyes, and spontaneously they broke into helpless laughter.

9

EARLY SUNDAY morning the police called Jane. The body of Charles Lawrence, *alias* Christopher Lansing, *alias* Chester Loring, *alias* Carl Lamb, was to be released for burial on Tuesday. Did Miss Forsyth have any instructions in the matter?

Yes, Jane said, she would defray the funeral expenses but she hoped there need be no regular service. In the circumstances it would only be a mockery and provide a field day for the news media. Anyhow, who would attend except for his two wives and, probably, the Toymans?

Jane sat staring at the telephone. Then she removed her wedding ring, holding it so she could read the tiny engraved inscription inside: "Eternal love. C.L." Perhaps, she thought, he got them cheaper by the dozen, but she felt no bitterness. All his gaiety, his good looks, his laughter, his swift passion, his charm were to be reduced to ashes. There would be nothing left of Chris. Whatever his real name, he would always be Chris to her. There was nothing but the pain and the heartbreak and the disillusionment he had left in his wake.

She shook her head as though trying to thrust away the vivid pictures of Chris that crowded her mind. People don't die for you suddenly, completely, even when you know they were never what you believed. They die little by little, in each thing you shared, in the small jokes, in words that bring back vivid memories. Not all at once.

She dropped her head on her arm and cried, not for the man whose body lay under the knife, but for the man he might have been, for the love and the happiness she had known. That at least had been real, even if mistaken.

At last she got up to bathe her face in cold water, feeling a little more at peace with herself. She had taken her last farewell of her dead.

As she came downstairs, Mike demanded, after a quick look at the telltale reddened eyes, "And where do you think you are going?"

"I thought I'd go up to the apartment and pack our things and tell the superintendent we won't be living there any more. Just sort of clear the decks."

"I'll go with you."

"I'd rather do this myself."

"Sure you would if you could have your druthers. But there's no point in you trying to take everything on your shoulders. Let's get cracking before it gets too hot."

"Jane," Forsyth called as he came into the hall, "I was just picking up the phone when your call came from the police. I listened in. I hope you don't mind. Then I called Cummins. He's all against having the funeral kept secret, no service, all that." Seeing his niece's rebellious face, he went on, "It makes you look vindictive or something. I know how you feel but I think you'd be wise to follow his suggestion."

"Provide a Roman holiday," she said in distaste. "Oh, all right, I'll call back."

"Actually, I've already done that," Forsyth said rather apologetically.

Jane struggled with her temper and then she turned away

and opened the door. Mike nodded reassuringly at Forsyth and then followed Jane out onto Park Avenue and hailed a cab.

The little basement apartment was stifling and Mike flung open the window. Jane looked around her. The table she had kept so carefully polished was gray with dust. Fingerprint powder probably. The drawers of the little cabinet she had found in a secondhand shop and painted to hold their clothes had been searched. Everything was upside-down. The curtain behind which hung dresses and suits had been pulled part way off the rod and one of Chris's suits had been thrown carelessly on the floor.

It was one which had just come back from the cleaner, Jane thought in dismay, and Chris would be expecting to wear it. No, he wouldn't want it again.

"Suppose you pack your own things," Mike said, "and I'll look after—his. You'll want to give them to the Salvation Army, I suppose."

"There's nothing of mine here I want to keep. All this stuff can go to the Salvation Army unless the superintendent can use it for his family. There's such a lot of them. He might want the furniture too."

"All right, I'll stack the clothes on the couch and call the superintendent. How about the rent?"

"It's paid until the end of the month. I'd better go through the food. Canned stuff I can leave but—" She opened the refrigerator. "Why, the butter and milk are still fresh! It seems forever since I was here. And the steak—" Tears welled up in her eyes. "We were going to celebrate his homecoming Friday. We always celebrated when he had a free weekend." She tried to laugh, wiping her eyes. "How silly to cry over a steak."

"I'll tell the superintendent about the food in the refrigerator and the canned stuff and arrange to have him clean the place when he's taken out whatever he wants."

Mike went down the hall to the back apartment and Jane heard his voice, heard the superintendent say, "That's mighty nice of Mrs. Lansing. We can sure use anything she doesn't need. My wife and I are sorry this terrible thing had to happen to her. Such a nice young couple. I'll go in and thank her myself."

"Perhaps you'd better not. This has been hard on her, you know. I'll turn the key over to you. If anything comes up, you can reach—uh, Mrs. Lansing at her uncle's house." He gave the name, address, and telephone number. Then apparently he gave the man an ample tip because there was a flustered, "Well, I'm sure that's very generous of you. I've done nothing to deserve it."

"Just don't answer any questions from the press if you can avoid it. You don't know anything about anything. Okay?"

"Sure, sure. Only I'm afraid it's a bit late. They came swarming around after the news got out and several of them came in to look around and talk to my wife."

The cabbie, who had been told to wait, was obviously relieved when they reappeared, having begun to suspect that his passengers had slipped away.

Only when they were back at the house did Mike make up his mind and take Jane into the drawing room, which was so little used. "I've got to talk to you. I realize Cummins is a wizard and the police know their job, but they probably have an eye on all of us and I know, at least, the ones who can be eliminated; you and Uncle Jim and I. So let's go over everything we know and see what turns up."

II

An hour later Jane leaned back in her chair with a sigh of exhaustion. "There is nothing more. Absolutely nothing."

Mike made no reply. The poor little kid had known nothing about the man she had married, nothing about his background, nothing about his family except what he had told her. Had anyone checked on his family?

He picked up the telephone and called the police. He identified himself and said that he was speaking for Miss Forsyth—or was it Mrs. Lansing? Did Charles Lawrence have any family in Buffalo, as he claimed, a lame mother and a mentally retarded sister? If so, Miss Forsyth thought they should be told of the funeral arrangements and some effort made to have them attend if they wished to do so. He smiled reassuringly into Jane's wide, startled eyes.

"I never even thought of them except just at first. I simply forgot."

Mike waved his hand to silence her, listened. Listened for some time. Then he said, "Thank you very much. I must say I think the police have done a brilliant job." Then he laughed.

He turned to Jane, smiling. "The policeman was surprised at getting any bouquets thrown at the department. Very much pleased." The smile faded. "Charles Lawrence had no family in Buffalo. Nearest they could come to it is a one-legged woman with an epileptic ten-year-old."

Jane shivered. "What horrible things happen to people. I never knew it."

"Well, you aren't going to take the troubles of the world on your shoulders. God knows there's enough pain and suffering and disappointment floating around. You can't deal with all of it. Anyhow, it appears that Charles Lawrence was born in Jersey City. Father deserted them when the kid was about eight. The mother didn't want the responsibility of bringing up the boy and she too vanished into the night. Some child care group looked after the boy until he was eighteen. Several people became foster parents because he was such an engaging little fellow, but they always brought him back. Couldn't cope with him. If he wasn't pilfering from them or their neighbors, he was in some other scrape. Just born with a twist in his nature, I guess. Even childless women who had applied for adoption gave him up."

"Mike! I ought to call Mrs. Toyman. She loved him like a son and her husband had such high hopes for Chris."

Raised voices on the street made Mike get up and look out of the window. Sunday strollers had gathered outside the Forsyth house, staring curiously at the windows behind which was the widow—or one of the widows—of a murdered man.

"Let's get out of here," he said sharply.

"What's wrong?"

"A flock of mindless Peeping Toms," he said savagely. "The kind of ghoul who drove Mrs. Kennedy away from the house in Georgetown where she tried to rebuild her life after the assassination of the President. We'll go through the garden and that office building on Lexington. Come on." He held out his hand and drew her to her feet. A warm, firm hand to which she found herself clinging. It was only Mike, of course, Mike who had always been there, teasing her, tormenting her, looking after her, Mike the dependable. But now Mike—different, somehow. For the first time in her life she felt self-conscious with him. She drew her hand away.

He was aware of the change in her; he had always been aware of any change in her, long before he had known that he was in love with her. For a moment he looked at her searchingly and then he said, "Okay, let's take it on the lam."

Uncle Jim was in his bookroom and he looked up from the desk at which he was writing as the two appeared in the garden. He opened the window.

"Got an audience out front," Mike called. "You might see

whether New York's Finest can push them back into the gutter. We're going out through the garden. You'll see us when you see us."

Forsyth nodded and reached for the telephone.

"Sometimes I get so mad at him for taking things out of my hands and making my decisions for me," Jane confessed, "but he's the Rock of Gibraltar, isn't he?"

"Now where?" Mike asked, when they had emerged safely and undetected into the lobby of the Lexington Avenue building.

"I'd like to see Mrs. Toyman. I owe her that much."

"Where does she live?"

"South Orange, New Jersey."

"Okay." Mike dug in his pocket for change, found a pay telephone in the lobby, and called the garage where he kept his car.

"It will be around in about a quarter of an hour. We might as well stay in here. It's cooler than the street."

Jane stood looking out. "How still it is!"

"Sunday morning. People are catching up on sleep or going to church or reading the papers."

They stood side by side, watching the street, an occasional bus, a few private cars that had room, once a week, to move in New York and even to park there. Once again Jane found herself conscious of Mike's nearness, though he did not touch her, did not speak to her. It was as though they were communicating without words, which was oddly disturbing, but something she would not willingly have ended.

Then Mike said, "There it is. Let's go." He tipped the driver and helped Jane into his little two-seater.

They drove across Manhattan to the Lincoln Tunnel and then, when they had turned onto the Jersey Turnpike, traffic picked up, vacationers heading for the Jersey shore, as months later they would be heading for Florida beaches.

America moving on. Once off the Turnpike there were suburban streets, people spilling out of churches onto the road, starting cars with a roar, crossing the street without looking in either direction.

Jane broke the silence between them by talking about the Toymans. "He is as fussy as a hen, but he manages his business very efficiently, Chris—Chris said. A sound and cautious businessman. And Mrs. Toyman—well, she reminds you of pictures of middle-aged women sitting on rocking chairs on the front porch mending or darning while they wait for the bread to bake. She should have had half a dozen children. Instead she is really the imagination behind the business. It has made for a fine marriage, people complementing each other."

"Is that," Mike asked, "your formula for a happy marriage?" and could have kicked himself.

To his relief she considered his question thoughtfully. "Part of it, I suppose, but I'd like to have something more —more romantic, I suppose."

More romantic. Mike was aware of the rush of blood up the back of his head. Hold it, Heald, he warned himself. There is no percentage in anger. But how anyone could do this to Jane, to little Jane, who was so trusting—who had been so trusting. Romance. Probably all her life Jane would be a little in love with that good-looking heel.

The Toyman house was on a tree-lined street, a big, square, old-fashioned house with a freshly painted white picket fence and a deep porch with cane-bottomed rocking chairs lined up like soldiers. A quiet street with cars parked at the curb, as if it had been designed before the day when garages were a necessity. The car in front of the Toyman house was, unexpectedly, a Bentley. An old car, but still a Bentley.

Mike whistled. "Toys must be profitable."

"Oh, they've had that for years and years. The original owner died or got too old to drive or something and was glad to get rid of it cheap."

"I hope we won't disgrace them," Mike said as he parked his little car behind the stately Bentley.

On the porch Jane nudged and pointed. The mailbox was shaped like an alligator with wide-open jaws into which the mail was dropped. The doorbell was a puppy with a sign, "Just pull my tail."

Obediently Mike tugged, and instead of chimes there was the sound of a dog barking. Really, he thought, Tricks for Tiny Tots could get out of hand.

The door was opened by a stout woman of forty-five wearing a big apron over a gray linen summer dress. As she opened the door, there was wafted the appetizing smell of roasting beef. A big midday Sunday dinner, Mike thought. Some people ran almost too much to type.

As she caught sight of Jane, the half-questioning smile prepared for a neighbor—she'd probably expected someone to drop in to borrow a cup of flour or an egg, Mike thought—changed. For a moment she stared mutely at the girl and then, wordlessly, she held out her arms, rocking Jane, crooning over her as though she were a baby.

Then she said, "Come in. Come in. Henry, here's Jane and—"

"My cousin. Michael Heald."

Toyman, as might be expected, sat with the Sunday paper scattered at his feet, working the crossword puzzle. He was in shirt sleeves and, with a sputter of tut-tuts, he slipped on his jacket and came to take Jane's hand in his own, patting it.

"Well, Marge," he said, "here's your girl at last."

"Yes. Excuse me while I baste the roast and put on the potatoes. It won't take a minute. Everything is ready.

You'll stay for dinner, of course."

"I'm sorry," Jane said. "We'd love to. Perhaps another time. But today I wanted to come. You've been—you were so kind to us both."

"Like a son to us," Toyman said heavily. "Wasn't he, Marge?" But she had already disappeared into the kitchen.

Mike looked around him. This, if he had ever seen one, was a room with a split personality. Against a heavy background of banal furniture, matched overstuffed pieces upholstered in dark green because a sensible color doesn't show dirt, had been superimposed a kind of display room for Toyman products. On the mantel there was a miniature magician in a black cloak lined with red satin, pulling a rabbit out of his tall hat. Beside it was a cabinet with a roll of colored streamers and the rest of the magician's bag of tricks. Mike itched to examine the toy, try out the tricks.

On a table beside a Tiffany lamp and, to his startled eyes, a family Bible with heavy brass hinges was a small bombing plane. This was more than Mike could withstand. Like any father who takes over his son's electric train on Christmas Day, he picked it up, wound it, and let it soar out of his hand, where it circled the room, dropped bombs, and then returned to the table.

Mike grinned. "Look at this, Jane!"

She responded to his enthusiasm. "I'll get you one for your birthday," she promised.

Toyman disapproved of this levity on a solemn occasion. It outraged his sense of fitness. "I suppose," he said, firmly returning to the matter at hand, "you'll want to know how Chris's affairs stand. I can't tell you exactly at the moment but by the first of the month there will be a tidy sum coming in from commissions. And more later, no doubt, from the stuff on consignment. If you need a little advance—"

"Oh, no. I came only because you both had been so kind."

"Jane would have come in any case," Mike said, "but actually we came away on impulse this morning. There was a mob of sightseers staring in the windows, so we had to get away."

"Horrible! As though you hadn't had enough. But we must all try to forget." He indicated a corner cupboard. "These are ideas Marge is still working on but hasn't really perfected yet. We don't usually show them to anyone until we've applied for a patent, but with Jane, of course—"

He displayed some ingenious mechanical toys. "Need some work yet but Marge will find the solution, of course. She always does."

Again the dog barked and Toyman glanced out of the window. Through the carefully draped white curtains could be seen a police car parked behind Mike's little two-seater. Across the street a boy on a bicycle had stopped to stare.

"Now what," Toyman began, annoyed, and went to open the door as his wife called, "Henry, will you go? I'm mixing the salad."

The dog barked before Toyman could open the door and the policeman stood staring.

"Yes, officer," Toyman said. "What can I do for you?"

"Just a few questions." As Toyman stood in the doorway, the policeman suggested, "It might be better if we talk inside. People are beginning to gather."

"Oh, of course. Of course. Come this way." He ushered the two uniformed men into the living room just as his wife came out of the kitchen, a faint aroma of garlic clinging to her person. She stood for a moment staring at them and then automatically wiped her hands on the big apron as she came forward.

"What is it, Henry?"

"You are Henry Toyman?" the spokesman for the two policemen asked.

"Yes."

"Do have the men sit down, Henry."

"Of course. Of course." Toyman looked around vaguely but the men stood waiting to be introduced to Mrs. Toyman.

"My wife. Mrs. Lansing. Mr. Held."

"Heald," Mike said.

At the word Lansing the policemen looked sharply at Jane in her sleeveless white dress and acknowledged the introduction to Mrs. Toyman.

"Officer Grant," the spokesman said. "Officer Morris." They sat down.

Mike noticed in amusement that the eyes of the younger man were drawn irresistibly to the little magician in his bright cape.

Mrs. Toyman stood twisting the hem of her apron in her hands until her husband gently pushed her into a chair and seated himself.

"A man known to you as Christopher Lansing was in your employ?"

Toyman nodded. "My best salesman. Like a son to me. Like a son. Wasn't he, Marge?"

Mrs. Toyman nodded without speaking. She was, Mike thought, the one who had the deepest devotion to the worthless young man who must have epitomized the family she had never had.

"Had you known him long?"

"A couple of years. He came just after my wife had planned this idea of expanding our stock, appealing to an older age group. We didn't know the best way to exploit the stuff, but Chris took to it like a duck to water. Well, when I tell you that I planned to turn the business over to him when I retire, you can imagine—"

"How did you get in touch with him?"

Toyman hesitated, unsure of the policeman's meaning.

"I mean did he come to you looking for a job or did you advertise or was he sent by an agency or by personal recommendation?"

"Oh, I advertised. I had—must have had twenty or more applicants. Picked him out of the crowd without any hesitation. At least, my wife did. She's got what you call flair. Real flair."

"I suppose you know he wasn't really Christopher Lansing." The officer glanced at Jane, who nodded.

"I know now. He was really Charles Lawrence."

"How long have you known that?"

"I found out yesterday from the police."

"I don't understand it!" Toyman exclaimed. "Don't understand it. Chris was the last, the very last— There has to be some mistake."

"No," Jane said quickly. "He married another woman under a different name seven months after he married me, a model called Beverly Barker. It was in the papers. I went to see her. I had to know. She's awfully pretty, but she's hard. When I saw her picture, I thought no one could compete with her, but when I met her I—didn't want to compete, and though she told the Manhattan police she had an alibi for the night Chris was killed, I don't think they believed her." She added expressionlessly, "Neither did I. But they are going to check everyone's alibi, everyone who knew him. I don't have one. I was just—waiting for him to come home. There's no proof, of course, so I've got to find some proof about other people. It's the only way I can clear myself. By elimination."

She was aware of Mike trying to catch her eye, Mike shaking his head in warning.

"Then you knew nothing about the man's background," Officer Grant said to Toyman.

"Nothing. Nothing at all. His—well, his whole personality carried its own guarantee."

"Would you know where he got a lot of new hundred-dollar bills? Two witnesses noticed them."

Toyman shook his head. "He just took orders, you know. He didn't collect for the merchandise. We did our own billing from the office, of course."

Now Jane saw Mike was signaling that it was time they left so that the police could carry on their interrogation without witnesses. She got up quickly. "Sorry, we must go. But we'll keep in touch. And if—the service will be on Tuesday at the funeral parlor. If you'd care to come—very private—and no flowers, please."

"Don't let me drive you away," Officer Grant said quickly. "I just wanted—routine matter the New York cops asked us to check on—checking on everyone, of course—doesn't mean a thing."

Mike's hand closed over Jane's arm, half in restraint, half in support, and she felt its warmth, felt its warning.

"I don't suppose you'd have any trouble accounting for your time Thursday night, actually Friday morning, say midnight to five?" Grant was smiling to indicate that the question was routine, meaningless.

Toyman stared at him, blinking, at a loss. It was Mrs. Toyman who shuddered. "I'll never forget that night! Henry had an abscessed tooth. Never saw such pain and no dentist available at that time of night, of course. And now you have to go to a specialist for extractions. Everyone has his own tiny specialty. It's a wonder to me—"

"So Mr. Toyman was home all night."

"He was indeed."

The policeman looked at notes. "Must have made a quick recovery. I see you attended a toymakers' annual convention on Friday."

"Henry always does what has to be done," his wife said.

93

10

MIKE AND Jane stopped at a small restaurant in New Jersey for club sandwiches and iced coffee and drove back slowly to New York, which was baking under the sun.

They did not speak but the silence between them was companionable and without strain. Mike glanced at Jane's profile, but she was deep in thought, far away from him. How long, he wondered, would it take her to get over Chris? At least she had no illusions about him, but she had been in love, deeply in love, for a year. And even when—or if— she recovered, there wouldn't be much chance for him. If you've regarded a guy as a brother for the past ten years, you aren't apt to think of him in any other way.

There was a frown drawing her brows together, a frown that deepened.

"What is it?" he asked.

"I don't know. Something that bothered me. Something—unexpected."

"At the Toymans', you mean?"

"I don't think so. Just something nibbling at the back of my mind. Something wrong."

There was plenty wrong, he agreed.

The hot breeze lifted Jane's hair. "This is the first summer Uncle Jim hasn't gone to Maine. I wonder why. Of course the town house is cool, but—"

"That's a big place up there," Mike said, "and without you and the crowd you always brought along, it didn't seem worthwhile opening the house."

"But he still had you. Oh, you're a working man now. At least—aren't you? You didn't give up your job on my account, did you? Oh, Mike, I'd hate that."

"You don't think a paper like the *Chronicle* would let a good man go, do you?" he said in shocked accents.

"Well—"

"The thing is I went to the City Editor and told him I was going to stick to this case until it was solved. I had some ideas about it. And darned if Ivan the Terrible didn't say he'd keep the job open for a month and see what happened if I'd give them an exclusive on anything I discovered."

"Really?"

"Cross my heart," he said solemnly.

She laughed and tucked her hand under his arm. "Do you think you'll find out anything?"

"I can try." As she lapsed into her troubled thoughts again, he said quickly, "Where would you start looking if it was up to you?"

He was relieved to see the change in her as she tackled a practical problem. "I'd start with the woman in the motel. The one who vanished. She's the key to everything, isn't she? If she didn't kill Chris, she must know who did."

"Has it occurred to you," Mike said suddenly, "that there may never have been a woman with him at the motel? Sure, he registered for Carl Lamb and wife, but no one saw the woman. There was no trace of her in the place."

"But why?"

"I don't know why. I've thought of half a dozen reasons: some man with whom he was planning a crooked deal and didn't dare risk meeting openly. That's the one I keep coming back to." Seeing Jane's incredulous expression, he agreed.

"Oh, I know it sounds like something the CIA would pull. Just the same, it happens. Not only in espionage, but in business deals, in dope peddling, in smuggling. And that's just for starters. For my money, the key isn't the vanishing Mrs. Lamb, it's the vanishing wallet with all its nice new money."

"Where could that money have come from, Mike? Mr. Toyman never paid him in cash. Anyhow you heard what he said, he paid Chris a token salary plus commissions, and he only got those once a month. It's nearly the end of the month now. And the money didn't come from Beverly Barker. I'm pretty sure of that. She's the kind who takes, not the kind who gives."

"They must have been two of a kind," Mike said with calculated brutality.

Jane winced and then she agreed. "So you can't help wondering about the money, after all." Her mouth twisted wryly. "With two wives and a job that kept him busy, Chris couldn't have had much time for—well, I keep coming back to the money. Where would a lot of money come from? Within the range of Chris's acquaintances, I mean. There's only Mrs. Fitch—" She caught her breath. "Oh!"

"Yes," Mike said quietly, "there is also Uncle Jim who is well heeled and loaded with motive. And I have a lot more money than I ever draw on."

Jane was silent for a long time. "But you would never, never in all the world, let anyone extort money from you."

"But," Mike pointed out, "Chris wasn't allowed to keep the money long, you know."

II

"Look," Detective Forman said, goaded by Mike's persistence, "we were running this department pretty well long before you tried to take a hand and give us the benefit of your vast experience. Suppose you leave it to us."

"Well, there are a few things that occurred to me." Mike was impervious to the detective's unconcealed impatience.

"A few things have occurred to us too."

"I can't help wondering about all that money the guy was flashing around the night he was killed. Where did he get it? Who took it?"

"We'd thought of that fact," Forman said dryly.

"Yes, of course." Mike sounded apologetic but he did not get up to leave. Instead he launched into his theory that it was a man and not a woman whom Lawrence had planned to meet secretly at the motel to arrange some sort of deal. Forman watched him, a curious expression on his face.

"I've been talking to the City Editor of the *Chronicle*. He finds you a hell of a lot more plausible than I do, Heald, but then—reporters!" There was a lifetime of bitterness in the detective's tone.

Mike grinned at him, settled himself more firmly in his chair. "Jane and I went over to see the Toymans yesterday. Chris, or whoever the hell he was, didn't get the money there."

Forman yawned.

"And there are a lot of alibis for that night I could bear to know about."

"You don't say. Be sure to confide in us when you find out anything. But I hope it will be a lot more convincing than the alibi you came up with for yourself."

For once Mike was out of countenance. "I know it is a stinker, but it is true. If you questioned those guys, one of them must have been sober enough to remember—and the taxi driver—"

Mike broke off when he saw that the detective was grinning widely.

"Cool it, Heald. We've run down four of your fellow sinners who remember pouring you into a taxi, and we've found the driver who brought you home and let you in, much against your wishes. You wanted to join Jacques Cousteau's crew on the *Calypso* and you put up some spirited resistance. Quite an epic. Man, you must have been loaded!"

"Why, you—" Mike laughed, mostly in relief.

"I thought I'd better put you out of your misery. Now if you'd have the kindness to get the hell out of here I could get down to some productive work. The Lawrence murder isn't the only case I'm working on, you know."

"About those alibis," Mike went on doggedly.

The detective leaned back in his chair, an expression of pained resignation on his face. "There's a lot to be said for the old system of putting a guy in irons and then throwing him in a dungeon. Kept him on ice until he was needed. Or at least it kept him quiet. I've often wondered why the police department doesn't try it out here."

Mike ignored this. "We have several possibilities. The first, of course, is this second wife. Jane saw her and told her she thought you didn't believe in her alibi. And then there is Mrs. Harrison Fitch."

"Good God!"

"Well, damn it, I don't like dragging the woman in if she is in the clear. But there is money somewhere, and when Jane saw her—"

There was no smile on the detective's face. "Miss Forsyth went to see Mrs. Fitch?"

"Well, she wondered—"

"Look, Heald, and listen to this. Get out of this case and stay out. You and Miss Forsyth are simply muddying the waters. We haven't overlooked Mrs. Fitch as a possibility, but it won't help our investigation to have you two tip her off to the fact that she is under suspicion. I mean that."

"Yes," Mike said almost meekly, "but Jane wanted to know the truth."

"She's not alone in that. Now do you get out or do I have you thrown out? There's one thing you kids seem to have overlooked. Murder. That's it. M U R D E R. Only the first one is hard. Only the first one matters. Jane Forsyth is getting herself entangled in a nasty mess—nastier than she has any conception of. She's asking for it, man! Tell her we don't want another corpse on our hands, not a nice girl like that."

Mike got up. "Just one more thing. Have you checked on Toyman's alibi for that night? I admit I don't see why he would kill a guy he seemed to like so much. His wife says he had an abscessed tooth and was home all night."

"Suppose," Forman said politely, "just suppose you come to see me first with any bright ideas, instead of going around asking people how suspicious their behavior might be. That's not a request. It's an order. Now—" He half rose.

"Okay. Okay. I'm on my way out. I've practically gone." Mike pushed back his chair. "Oh, one more thing, about the weapon that might have killed Chris—" He took in Forman's expression and went out hastily, closing the door behind him.

"Damned kids," Forman grumbled to himself, and then he grinned as he recalled Mike's relief when he realized that his alibi held up. Now that must have been a party to end parties.

He pushed aside his IN basket at which he had been working when Mike appeared, pulled a scratch-pad toward him and wrote *Mrs. Harrison Fitch*. He decorated the word with some fancy scrollwork. Not, of course, that the woman would have been fool enough to fall for Lawrence's blandishments or his threats a second time. Then he noted Mike's suggestion that Lawrence's appointment at the motel had been with a man. Crooked deal of some sort. A man who was paid off in cash or stole it from the dead body. Could be. But at this point anything was possible.

He went through reports, reread the testimony of the drive-it-yourself man and the night clerk at the motel. Both of them had seen the wallet bulging with new hundred-dollar bills. It was late now, of course. The murder had occurred early Friday morning and it was Monday. Chances were the money had been deposited. Nonetheless he called for Sergeant Purcell and asked him to see the two witnesses and find out whether by any remote chance the money was still in their possession. If the new bills had been issued in sequence, there might be a useful lead.

He made a note to find out where Mrs. Fitch banked and learn, if possible, whether she had made any heavy withdrawal in hundred-dollar bills. There should be some record, but whether the information would be forthcoming was another point. Banks were not willing to give out information regarding their depositors. What he needed was a man high up in the financial world who carried some weight.

Well, of course, there was James Forsyth, former member of the Stock Exchange, highly respected. Discreet investigations, and investigations were discreet with men in Forsyth's position, revealed that he had rejected more than one offer of a high government post. An impeccable record. He carried a lot of influence.

Forman reached for the phone and then drew his hand back. There was no one who had been more anxious than Forsyth to see the marriage of Jane Forsyth and Lawrence break up. Lawrence was not the kind who would show any false modesty or reluctance about being paid off. Probably he had been hoping for that ever since he learned that Jane would not come into her money until he had proved himself to be a responsible citizen.

Or perhaps, and Forman left his imagination free to drift, Forsyth had persuaded Lawrence, for a suitable fee, to register at the motel with a woman, be discovered, and provide Jane with evidence for a divorce. Then, when the unsuspecting man had gone to sleep, half drunk according to the autopsy report, the woman planted by Forsyth had admitted him and—

"Oh, nuts," Forman said in disgust, startling an officer who was coming into the small office.

11

THE VOICE was a husky whisper as though the speaker had a bad cold. "Miss Forsyth? I can tell you what happened to your husband."

"Who are you?"

"I was a friend of his a while back, but he got in too deep for me. I wanted out."

"Please tell me."

"Look, I've got a record," the whispering voice said. "I'm not talking to the police."

"Then come here. I won't tell anyone, but I've got to know, and so many people are under suspicion now that it is only fair. Please come."

"Will you walk into my parlor? Not me. There's a movie in the Bronx." The voice explained how to get there. "Sit in an aisle seat in the next to the last row. I'll meet you there in—let's see—an hour. I have ten-fifteen. Check your watch."

"This afternoon I'm going to Chris's funeral service. I have to be there at two o'clock. Can you make it tomorrow morning?"

"Now or never. I'm taking enough risk as it is."

Jane pushed back the telephone. She was excited, but she was uncertain too. One thing sure, Uncle Jim would never let her keep this unorthodox appointment, but if she didn't, she might lose her only opportunity to clear up the mystery of Chris's death.

She looked at herself in the mirror. She wore a thin black dress and in her black handbag she had tucked a square of black lace to wear over her head for the service. At the door she turned back and scrawled a note for her uncle, telling him about the telephone call, the instructions she had been given, and saying she would be back in time for the service.

The doorman from the building next door got her a cab and she gave the address. It seemed a long way to the movie theater in the Bronx and she kept consulting her watch anxiously. It was a few minutes after eleven when she dismissed the taxi and bought a ticket at the theater. An incurious woman in the booth took her money and change rattled down.

There were no ushers, but none were needed. There weren't more than half a dozen people in the theater, a mother with five noisy children sitting well down front.

Jane found a seat in the next to the last row on the aisle and waited for her eyes to adjust to the darkness after the bright light of the street. But before she could make the adjustment, a hand came down over her mouth from the back row, a needle was thrust into her arm.

When she awakened, she had to fight an attack of nausea and then she was aware that she was in the trunk of a car, lying on something that jabbed into her ribs, a tire iron or some tool. She was curled up away from the opening. A hand held her down, preventing her from turning.

"Busybody," the voice whispered. "You'll be here until you rot. This house has been unoccupied for over a year and there's nothing on either side. And that gag will keep you from making a sound. You'll be joining your boyfriend in hell."

The trunk lid banged down and then there was another

sound, a scraping sound that ended with a thud. A rusty garage door had been closed.

Jane lay in darkness, in the airless sweltering heat, head throbbing, stomach churning, tears spilling down her cheeks. To die like this! Trussed up like a chicken. And all of a sudden she was blazingly angry and no longer paralyzed by fear.

She had stumbled on something, frightened someone. But what had she learned that could conceivably be dangerous to anyone? She went over the list: Beverly Barker, Mrs. Harrison Fitch, the Toymans. There were so few possibilities, that is with people with whom she had been in contact. And not one of them could have managed to kidnap her, drag her out of the theater unconscious and unseen. It didn't make sense.

Her hands were tied behind her and she strained in vain to break the cord that held them. She could not call out. She shifted her position painfully and tried to kick on the lid of the trunk. She had so little leverage the result was only a faint tapping that no one would have noticed, even if the car had been parked on a street instead of in a garage, the closed garage of an unoccupied house.

There was no clue for anyone to follow. She had left a letter but that would lead Mike only as far as the theater. It was a dead end. Hours might pass before her letter was found. No, they'd surely look for her when the time came to go to the service for Chris.

Mike, she cried in her mind. Please find me, Mike. Please get me out. She made a final attempt to kick at the trunk lid, but there was so little air that she soon gave up, exhausted, drenched with perspiration, gasping for breath. She lay still, her futile attempt to call for help abandoned. She cried, the tears wet on her cheeks.

II

The call came through at noon. Mike stretched out his hand, after an inquiring look at Forsyth, and answered it.

"Mr. Heald?"

"This is Heald speaking." He listened, frowning. "Speak up, can't you? I don't understand you."

From his favorite chair Forsyth looked up alertly as he heard the strain in Mike's voice. Mike signaled frantically, covered the mouthpiece. "Get on another phone. Hurry, for God's sake. I'll keep him talking while you get the police. They have Jane."

Forsyth, without a word, ran to the kitchen where he seized the telephone.

"What do you want me to do?" Mike asked, trying to keep the whispering man on the phone.

"I told you. We've got the girl. Drop your interference and call off the police or she will die." The connection was broken.

Mike sat staring numbly at the silent phone. In a few minutes Forsyth came back. "I got the police."

"They wouldn't have time to trace the call."

"What did he say?"

Mike told him. "Whose toes did we step on?"

"This man—"

"Man or woman. The voice was so muffled I could hardly make out the words. Somewhere we got too close."

"They have Jane. What would have made her leave the house that way without telling anyone?"

Mike ran up the stairs to Jane's suite. The note was propped against the lamp in her sitting room, and he ripped it open, ran down to the bookroom.

"A movie in the Bronx. At least that's a place to start."

Forsyth reached for the telephone.

"Don't do that. You'll endanger Jane."

"What the hell do you think is happening to her right now?" For the first time Forsyth glared at Mike. "Neither of you had any business interfering. This is a police job." He put through the call and related what had happened. Even at this time his voice was under control, his explanation clear and succinct.

Before the two men could call a taxi, a police car drew up at the door and Forman signaled. They ran down the stairs and climbed in.

"Now talk," Forman said as the police car, siren screaming, lights blinking, raced toward the Bronx.

Mike read him the note and again told about the telephone call. Forman had little comfort to offer. "I warned you that you were playing with murder. Out of your weight. You and the girl both. She was asking for trouble. All this talk of slibis. Why," and the detective almost wailed, "won't people let the police handle their jobs without interference?"

Forsyth brushed that aside. "What are Jane's chances?"

"God knows. Oh, we'll find her in the long run, but—"

"Do you think they'll kill her?"

"They have killed once. But we'll get them. In the long run we'll get them. My grandmother was Swiss and she said they have a saying: 'Every door has a slippery step.' It takes only one slip."

The sleepy cashier at the movie came wide awake when she saw the police car, but she was of no help. "It's one of those sex movies. Won't get a real crowd until night, except for some fool woman bringing her kids just to keep them quiet, and they probably won't know what it's all about. I hope."

"You didn't see a young girl dressed in black?"

"I don't notice them, Officer. For a feature like this one, X-rated, most of them come in so furtively I get sick of watching them. . . . Oh, sure you can look around. But don't make any disturbance."

The four men went inside but, though a few teen-agers had been added to the audience, the place was still practically empty. One of the policemen checked both washrooms. The next to the last row on the aisle, where Jane had been instructed to sit, was their first goal, but there was only an empty seat. She had dropped nothing, left no sign of what had happened.

"Probably taken by surprise," Forman said. He spoke to the cashier again. "We're going to rope off the last two rows until we can get a fingerprint crew in here."

"It won't do you any good. That's where the kids like to do their lovemaking. They'll slide under any rope you put up."

"Then we'll put a man on guard until we've finished here." Forman went out to the car radio to issue orders.

"She must have been knocked out," Forman said. "Otherwise she'd have kicked up a fuss. But if she was unconscious, there had to be a car handy."

The cashier, willing to be helpful but not knowing how, said she had not noticed any car stop at the theater. But then she wouldn't, she confessed. She was knitting an afghan for her daughter's baby and following an intricate pattern, counting and all. She didn't pay attention to traffic. Why should she?

"What do we do next?" Forsyth asked, helpless, ravaged, for once not in control of a situation.

"You go home." As neither Forsyth nor Mike showed any disposition to leave the last spot where Jane was known to have been, Forman said, "There may be a message. Bound to be a message."

"Why?" Forsyth asked in discouragement.

"There's money in the background. Remember that missing billfold? Someone is going to try to collect when you are scared enough. You should be getting a demand sooner or later."

"You think she's alive then?" Forsyth said eagerly.

"Well," Forman did not commit himself, "she's valuable property. More valuable alive than dead."

"Is she?" Mike said somberly. "If they get their money, what have they to gain by setting her free?"

"We don't have much choice," Forman said bluntly. "Go on home. I'll send word to have your phone tapped in case someone tries to reach you that way."

III

Stan Wiltshire stood a little outside the gang, a looker-on, as he had always been a looker-on. Not that he expected equal treatment. Born with a harelip, he had spent all his seventeen years as an object of curiosity, ridicule, and cruelty by his peers. Only the couple paid by the state to house and feed him accepted him without comment, if without affection. The gang, which held undisputed leadership in the south Bronx, with a proud record for sabotage, arson, pocket-picking, burglary, and mugging, ignored him. Now and then they condescendingly permitted him to run their errands.

It wasn't that Stan expected equal treatment. He didn't expect to be a real member. He just wanted to belong to something, though he winced away from violence and could not bring himself to stone store windows and slash tires. It was stupid, vindictive business, the work of kids who couldn't make it in school, who tried to destroy their world. Stan knew humbly that he stood at the top of his class, which, in itself, was one reason for their contempt. Books! It was being eternally alien that was breaking him down.

This was the fifth time he had asked, metaphorically with his hat in his hand, to be given a real job, something worthy of their respect. His request was met with some laughter, some jeers.

"Okay," Mitch Burger said wearily, "you want to join the club you got to obey the rules."

"I'll do that," Stan said eagerly.

The boys exchanged glances, sniggered.

"First thing you got to do is to snatch a car," Mitch said in an authoritative tone. "Drive it up to Poughkeepsie to that garage we use as a drop. You've seen us get a car unlocked often enough. When they report back to us that you've made delivery, you're in."

"How would they know I'm from your outfit?"

There was a spontaneous roar of laughter. "You! How many guys go around with a face like that? What do you call it, harelip? God! They'd know you all right."

Mitch turned on his heel and swaggered off, followed by his faithful and admiring henchmen, and Stan was left alone. He knew as well as they did that they did not expect him to carry through. But they did not know of his desperation, his need to be one of them, one of something.

He set out on foot, his heartbeat accelerating, feeling a little sick with apprehension and with something else—a distaste for the thing he was going to do. If only it had been enough to do well in school, to be at the head of his class, and so easily. But it had not counted at all. Not with the gang that terrorized the south Bronx, the power symbol to the youth of the whole section.

He went past the movie theater, which displayed X-rated pictures, but he did not even stop, as usual, to look, embarrassed and fascinated, at the posters outside. He had his eyes on the cars parked at the curb. He noticed the patrolman sauntering past and hurried away. He needed a quieter street, a neighborhood street where most of the inhabitants would be at work.

At first he was discouraged, and at the same time oddly relieved. There were blocks of burned-out buildings, shells that had housed people and had been destroyed for insurance or destruction for its own sweet sake. But that was stupid, Stan thought rebelliously. It's making that counts, not tearing down. But who would give him a chance to make anything? With his face. All his life people had stared, showed revulsion, disgust, embarrassment. They tried not to look at him when they had to talk to him, even his teachers.

He trudged on, found a street of mixed breed, apartment houses, a couple of old private houses, a delicatessen, a cleaning establishment, a beauty parlor. One of the houses had a ROOMS FOR RENT sign in the window. The other actually had a private garage, but the house itself was run-down, there was a broken windowpane on the first floor. No chance of finding a car here.

He glanced around but there was no one in sight. He opened the garage door, which squeaked a protest, and there inside was a shabby old car. Probably, he told himself hopefully, it was a breakdown. It wouldn't run. But there was a key in the lock and the motor started at once. Well, he was in for it now. He had driven only twice before, each time in a stolen car acquired by one of the gang. They had let him drive it because it was too hot for them to handle.

He backed the car out gingerly, hit the curb, retrieved his position and headed for a main highway that would lead him eventually to New York Route 22 and the turnoff for Poughkeepsie.

He had left the Bronx now and he was headed upstate. So far so good. When he reached the garage and made delivery of the stolen car, he'd be admitted to the gang; they'd have to admit him. But he felt no triumph at all. If there was any other choice, any other way he could assert himself, prove himself, become a person in spite of his disfigurement—

He had to stop for a light at the road leading up to the *Reader's Digest* buildings. There was no one else in sight on the Saw Mill River Parkway. In the silence he heard a faint tapping. It sounded to him as though there was something wrong with the motor and Stan knew nothing about cars and what made them go. He heard it again: tap—tap—tap. But the car was not in motion. There was something in the trunk.

Stan's physical reactions were slow but his mental reactions were quick. When the light turned, he left the road for a smaller side road and pulled off. He slid out from under the wheel and went around to the trunk. There was the tapping again. He hesitated only a moment. Then, with a swift look around, he unlocked the trunk and opened it.

The girl lay on her side, her back turned to him, a gag around her head biting into her cheeks, her hands tied behind her. Oh, man! He had walked right into a kidnaping or something worse. Stan wanted to take to his heels. Then he looked at the helpless girl and turned her over with gentle hands, looked into wide, terrified eyes. More terrified when they had taken in his disfigured mouth.

"It's okay," he told her. "Okay." He pulled out his pocketknife and cut the cord around her hands, removed the gag from her mouth with its swollen lips. He rubbed her wrists and when she tried to pull her hands away, he heard her cry out with pain because of the strained muscles in her shoulders.

"It's all right," he said, as though reassuring a small child, though no one had ever, in his memory, attempted to comfort him.

"Why did you do it?" she asked.

"I just found you, miss. I don't know who put you there."

"Isn't this your car?"

He swallowed. "No, I was just driving it for someone else." He looked into the wide, searching eyes. "I stole it," he burst out. "They said that was how I could get into the gang."

"Did you want to?" Jane was interested; she seemed more interested in his point of view than in the disfigured mouth that put people off.

"No, I didn't, but it's only guys like that who would have anything to do with me at all. Well, I mean, look at me!"

"You don't need to be a thief. All you need is some plastic surgery."

"And where would I get that kind of money? Anyhow, all bets are off. I'll have a record now. Car theft. I'm calling the police."

"Oh, would you do that?"

"Well, if you have any change. I'm sort of short."

"Take my purse. It's under me."

He stared at her, then he opened the purse and took out some change. He returned the rest to her. "I'll be right back," he promised. "Right back. Here, I'll help you out and you can sit in the front seat. You'd be more comfortable. I—" He thrust the car keys into her hand. "You don't have to wait for me if you don't want to."

She smiled at him. "I'll wait. Call my uncle first." She gave him the number. "Then the police, Homicide division. Try to get a message through to Detective Forman, will you, but I guess anyone will do. Say it is Jane Forsyth."

The boy ran down the lane and into town, looking for a public telephone. Jane, who had crawled into the front seat with his help, looked thoughtfully at the keys he had handed her, and then settled back to wait. Now that she was safe, she had something else to occupy her. All the troubles of the world, Mike had scoffed. But Mike hadn't seen the face that was ruining the life of a nice boy, at least a boy who could be nice if given half a chance.

He came running back and paused in surprise when he saw that she was waiting. "You trusted me."

"You saved me," she pointed out. "What's your name?"

"Stan Wiltshire." He was seventeen and he was at the head of his class. He'd been offered a scholarship from a minor college but he didn't know—maybe he should try something where he wouldn't scare people.

"You don't scare me," Jane said. "I'm just grateful. And wait until my uncle knows what you did! Just wait!"

"Wait until the police know," Stan said in disillusionment.

"And if you dare call them pigs or fuzz, you can get right out of this car," Jane stormed. And suddenly Stan found himself laughing. Actually laughing.

12

THE POLICE CAR, lights flashing, siren screaming, jolted to a stop beside the old jalopy in which Jane and Stan were talking quietly and earnestly. The two men from the Parkway police jumped out and ran to the car, guns drawn. Behind them Mike and a breathless Forsyth spilled out of the car.

The car door was flung open. "Out!" one of the policeman said, jerking his head.

"Now you just wait," Jane cried, her hand on the boy's arm, aware of his shrinking, his fear. "You let him alone. He's the one who saved me and called the police; at least it was the Manhattan police, but I guess they have no jurisdiction here—and he can't go back to the south Bronx because of what that gang would do to him. You let him alone!"

"Are you Jane Forsyth?" the policeman asked as the two men sheathed their revolvers.

"Yes, I am and—oh, Mike!" She tumbled out of the car and into his arms.

For a moment he held her in a crushing grip and then he held her back to look at the tearstained face, the swollen mouth with its dry lips. "It's okay, kid. It's all right, baby."

"I know. I knew you'd find me but I didn't know when, and it was awful in that trunk without any air and a gag and my hands tied behind my back and nothing I could do but kick at the lid of the trunk, and with the garage door closed—" She turned to smile at Forsyth, who gave her a quick hug and a light kiss on the cheek.

"You've had us in quite a spin," he said lightly.

"All right," the highway policeman said, "let's have it." He sent his partner back to the car to report by radio. "Manhattan Homicide was pretty urgent. We picked up these men at the line."

Jane described the telephone call, telling her that the caller knew who had killed her husband. He said he was afraid to have the police intervene because he had a record and he wouldn't come to the house.

"So we agreed to meet at the movie theater. You found my note?"

Mike nodded.

"Well, I did just what he said, and took a seat on the aisle in the next to last row. It was dark and my eyes hadn't adjusted yet and then—right away—a hand came over my mouth from the back row and I felt a needle in my arm."

She had awakened in the trunk of the car, gagged and with her hands bound, and she had heard the garage door close.

"For a minute—just a minute—I thought no one would ever find me." Her voice shook. "And then, as long as I could breathe I kept kicking at the lid, thinking maybe someone would hear me. But I could do it only a little at a time because of the air. Well, then the garage door opened, it squeaked awfully, and the car started and we drove a long way, at least it seemed like a long way, and then it stopped. So I kicked again. I had to do something."

The policemen exchanged looks. Quite a kid. Scared but not scared out of her wits. Not by a long shot.

"So then the trunk was unlocked and Stan—this is Stan Wiltshire—cut the gag and the cords and rubbed my hands until the circulation came back, and he ran to call Uncle Jim and the police and tell them where I was and that I was all right. And," she added, looking half defiantly, half pleadingly, "he took only enough money for the calls and gave me back the rest and he helped me into the front seat and he left me the car keys in case I didn't want to wait for him or didn't trust him, because of his face, you see. And that's why he had stolen the car," she rushed on, silencing Stan with a little gesture. "He's a foster child and the state supports him until he is eighteen, and he is the head of his class and he has a chance to go to college and a scholarship because he's so bright, only, because of the harelip—and that's why he took the car, so the gang would accept him. He's so dumb he thought no one else would. But they would, wouldn't they, Uncle Jim? And if you'd advance some of my money now, Stan could have plastic surgery. Oh, please, Uncle Jim!"

"You standing up for this gangster? This kidnaper?" the highway policeman was baffled.

"He didn't hurt me. He saved me. I told you that." She added kindly, "You just weren't listening, I suppose. And he's not a gangster. And after calling the police, the gang would—I don't know what they would do if they got hold of him. We owe him something, Uncle Jim." She shook his arm. "We owe him something."

"All right, dear. All right. Don't get so upset. We'll look into Stan's background, find out what we can, and if it's the way he says, we'll see the gang doesn't touch him and that he gets the surgical treatment he needs. And now suppose we get you home and put you to bed."

"I don't want to go to bed. I want just terribly to have a long drink of ice-cold water. My mouth is so dry and I'm so thirsty. And then I must go to the service." She looked at her watch. "It's after one. We'll have to hurry."

There was a hurried consultation between Forsyth and the police. Then the latter called a taxi. Jane hung back as Mike tried to help her in. "What about Stan?"

"We'll check him out," one of the policemen assured her.

Jane held out her hand. "Thank you, Stan. I'll never forget what you did. You're the bravest—"

"Don't get me wrong, miss. I was scared silly."

"That's why I think you are brave. And don't forget," she instructed the police severely, "that if you let him go back he'll be in danger."

"Stop worrying, Jane," Forsyth said. "The police will check out his story and if he's telling the truth, we'll arrange about plastic surgery. I know one of the top men and he may have Stan in shape for college by fall."

Stan stood looking from face to face, in disbelief, in wonder.

"What's your special interest?" Mike asked.

Color burned in the boy's face. This was the hardest confession of all. "Illustrating children's books," he mumbled. "I used to do it for fun, with library books. I didn't," he added in horror, "draw *in* the books."

Forsyth laughed aloud. "All right, Rembrandt, we'll see what can be done." He pressed the boy's shoulder and this time Jane got into the car without further delay, but she sat between the two men, clutching a hand of each all the way back to the city.

II

There was a mob outside the funeral parlor and Forsyth cursed under his breath. "You don't need to go through with this, you know," he told Jane.

"Of course I'm going through with it." She put the square of black lace over her hair and walked between Forsyth and Mike toward the entrance. After a look at them a policeman, one of three holding back the crowd of spectators, opened a path for them.

A microphone was thrust into Jane's face. "How do you feel about your husband's other wife?"

Forsyth caught Mike's arm and forced it down. "Don't provide a field day for the press," he muttered. "Keep your head, Mike."

"What are your future plans, Miss Forsyth?" a woman reporter called.

Jane, her head high, her face colorless, walked toward the door, which one of the funeral directors opened for her after a cautious inspection. Inside, an organ throbbed softly, playing "Nearer, my God, to thee." All at once, Jane found herself thinking how Chris would have roared with laughter and she was shaken by a nervous giggle.

Forsyth steered her into a seat in the front row that had been reserved for her, and where she was flanked by Forsyth and Mike. It was a funeral attendant who read a brief service, intoning the words in a meaningless jumble. Jane saw that only a few people had been admitted, probably either on Forsyth's instructions or on orders from the police. There was a spray of white roses on the dark wood of the casket and Jane wondered who had sent it.

A scent of heavy perfume made her look around and she saw Beverly Barker, not only in a black dress, but wearing a widow's veil that covered head and shoulders and fell to her waist. Her long strawberry blond hair swung loose and was more spectacular than ever against the black of her dress.

Someone was sobbing and trying to stifle the sounds. That was Mrs. Toyman, also in black, a heavy linen dress with long sleeves that, in the heat, was making her perspire. But it was probably the only black dress she owned, Jane thought in pity. Beside her, a black armband on his sleeve, sat Henry Toyman, his eyes fixed on the casket behind which the attendant stood, reading from the Bible. He removed his bifocals, wiped them, blew his nose, and then patted his wife's arm gently.

Someone still cares, Chris, Jane said silently to the unseen body in the casket. She wished that she could weep for him, but the Chris she had loved had no existence. Instead she found herself worrying about Stan Wiltshire, who had so much excuse to be crooked and who, when the test came, could not do it. What made one man honorable and marred another?

The service ended when the attendant clapped the Bible shut and was startled by the noise it made in the quiet room, and then the organ picked up its cue, playing the funeral music from Chopin's second sonata, and this time Jane found tears stinging her eyes and wiped them away, aware of the concerned looks of her two escorts. She wanted to explain that it was the music, which always made her cry, as she cried when she heard "Taps." She didn't want to make a dishonest appeal for sympathy.

As they rose from their place, Jane took one farewell look at the casket and turned away to encounter Beverly Barker, whose eyes were red and swollen.

"You didn't even send any flowers," she said accusingly.

Forsyth and Mike closed in on Jane.

Beverly laughed. "You sure bring your bodyguards. Full house out there, isn't it? You'll see pictures of me in the papers tomorrow, maybe on television tonight. A lot of them thought I was Number One Wife. I guess," and she smiled, "that's what Chester thought too."

Mike's hand tightened on Jane's arm, hurting her, but after a glance at his face, seeing that he was in the throes of one of his rare rages, she allowed him to lead her away without protest.

"That—that—"

"It doesn't matter, Mike," she told him. "She didn't hurt me. She couldn't hurt me." She turned as she saw the stout woman and the elderly man getting slowly to their feet.

"Mrs. Toyman!"

"Of course we came," Toyman said in a hushed tone, suited to his surroundings. "Of course. Are you all right, my dear?"

"Well—" Jane was aware that her dress was rumpled and dusty from lying on the floor of the car trunk, that she must look drawn and exhausted. But this was no time for explanations. "It's a strain," she said, and was aware of the inadequacy of her remark.

"This is a sad day for us, too. A terrible day. A terrible loss. Hard on Marge, too. Like losing a son."

Jane leaned forward impulsively and kissed the older woman's cheek. "You shouldn't have tried to come."

"I had to say good-bye," Mrs. Toyman said simply. "So much youth and life, all snuffed out, and no one even punished for it."

A tall, heavily built woman in a thin black dress and a small black hat, dark glasses covering her eyes, even in this twilit room, paused as she heard Mrs. Toyman's words, and then went swiftly past to the exit. Jane's eyes followed her. There was something familiar—oh, dear God! It must be Mrs. Fitch. It couldn't be. Then she saw Forsyth's start as he recognized her. But what had brought her here, taking a risk of being recognized? Was she too saying a last good-bye? Or was it curiosity?

As Jane reached the door, following Mrs. Fitch's hasty steps, a dark figure moved away from the door and became Detective Forman, wearing a dark suit and white shirt and looking like the chief mourner. But it was not to Jane he spoke; it was to Forsyth.

"I heard from the highway police that the girl is safe. I

didn't get the straight story about the boy."

"He's all right, I think."

"He'll be carefully checked out. Was Miss Forsyth hurt? She looks pretty good for a girl who has been doped, bound, gagged, locked in a car trunk. She seems fragile but there must be steel somewhere in her. We're getting her out the back way. I have someone in an unmarked car I want her to meet."

"Who's that?"

"Her bodyguard," Forman said grimly. "After this little episode we are taking no more chances on Miss Forsyth's impulses, however well meant. This way please."

At his direction they circled back past the improvised altar and the casket and through a side door to where a car was waiting. The man at the wheel was in plain clothes, so was the woman who was standing beside the back door, a short, squat woman with the face of a benevolent trained nurse, a forceful jaw, watchful eyes, and bulging forearms. She carried a big handbag.

"This, Miss Forsyth," Forman said, "is Hilda Talent, Mrs. Talent. She's one of our most experienced policewomen and one of our best shots. She is going to be with you at all times until we get the joker who killed Lawrence and had you abducted today."

He saw the rebellious twist of the girl's mouth. "We mean business, Miss Forsyth. This is for your own protection. You can accept it gracefully or—"

Forsyth intervened. "Jane is most grateful," he said blandly. As the policewoman let Jane precede her into the car, he looked at Mike. There was no room for a sixth passenger.

"That's okay," Mike said. "I have a date, anyhow. See you later." He walked away quickly and Forsyth got in the back seat beside the policewoman.

Before taking the seat beside the driver, Forman looked after Mike thoughtfully. "It would be a relief to my mind to know what he is up to now."

"He has a good head on his shoulders," Forsyth remarked.

"And he has a temper like a bull with a dozen darts in him," Forman said. He looked at Forsyth and laughed. "You think I'm blind? If I didn't have three—four—separate witnesses to the fact he was stoned the night Lawrence was killed, I'd have the handcuffs on him." He added, "Not but what three of them were his friends and the fourth—for a nice tempting fee— Oh, the hell with it! We'll meet trouble when it comes."

He nodded to the driver and the car slid into traffic.

13

IRVING BERNSTEIN, City Editor of the *Chronicle,* was known to the staff as Ivan the Terrible. He was listening on the telephone and doodling with his free hand when Mike went into his office, brushed papers off a chair, and sat down.

Bernstein pushed away the telephone, lighted a cigarette, saw that he already had one burning on the ashtray, and grunted, "I smoke too damned much."

As he was known to make this comment at least a dozen times a day and remained a chain smoker, Mike paid no attention.

"Well?" Bernstein said. "I don't suppose you came in here, upsetting my papers," he never knew where anything was, "just to do your yoga exercises. Though, like the man said, your periods of silence make your speech more bearable." As he talked he took in the drawn face of the young reporter. Looked as though he'd had a hard night. Then he remembered why Mike had asked to devote himself to an investigation into the murder of his cousin's husband.

"How are you making out?" he asked quietly. "Looks to me as though you're overdoing it."

In spite of all the bitter remarks made about the City Editor, Mike had found him understanding, and surprisingly enough, exceptionally patient. He was also a man of his word. While he had told Mike he could take a month for his investigations provided he produced an exclusive story, he had not really expected any results. The police knew their job and amateur detection did not impress him. It had been Mike's haggard expression that had influenced his decision.

And now, though Mike was aware of the horror Forsyth's criminal lawyer would feel at confiding in a newspaperman, he knew that whatever he had to say would remain secret until it was safe to print.

"This morning my cousin was kidnaped," he said.

Bernstein sat back and lifted his cigarette. "Fire when ready."

Mike told him the whole story, the telephone call in an unrecognizable voice saying Jane would be killed if they did not stop interfering. They were to call off the police. The discovery of Jane's note, the abortive trip to the theater, the call to Forsyth and then to the police from a young man who apparently had become involved in the story somehow, and Jane's story of being drugged, gagged, tied, and locked in the trunk of a car.

"Your cousin has had the hell of a few days," Bernstein commented. "She must be a nervous wreck."

"All she cared about was seeing that that kid who rescued her got a break; she wanted Uncle Jim to advance enough of her own money to provide him with plastic surgery. He has a harelip. And then she shook off the dust from the car and went straight to the service for—for that louse Lawrence." After a moment Mike said, "The other wife was there too, simply dripping with widow's weeds. She made some very nasty comments to Jane."

When he appeared to have ground to a stop, Bernstein said, "That's quite a story. Unexpectedly he smiled. "Don't worry. We won't use it as long as the police want it kept under wraps. We play along. But what protection is being provided for Miss Forsyth?"

"I'm moving back to the house this afternoon and a policewoman has been stationed there to be with Jane at all times. Uncle Jim's houseman has been armed. He's a veteran of World War Two and highly reliable. Not trigger-happy."

Again Bernstein nodded. "It looks as though either you or Miss Forsyth got too close to something."

"That," Mike admitted, "is what has me climbing the wall. I don't know who killed Lawrence. Jane doesn't know. Not a clue. Not a hint. Nothing. But we've got someone scared, someone who, except for the most unforeseen accident, would have let Jane die today."

"Well," and after Mike's excitement the City Editor sounded practical and down-to-earth, "according to you, she ran around assuring everyone that she was helping to check out alibis. She indicated she had her own sources. Oh, I know that's probably not the way she put it; that's a crude old newspaper man's jargon."

"Somehow," Mike said, "I don't think we've come anywhere near the truth yet. We've got two women who have surfaced: the second wife who, believe me, is a witch and tough as they come; and Mrs. Fitch. We have that missing wallet full of money. Where did it come from? The second wife doesn't fit, but Mrs. Fitch is loaded."

"If there are two women, there could be more, and there must be men involved with the women."

"The only one we've heard of is the agent with whom Beverly Barker claims to have been working at the time Chris or Lawrence—I can't sort out the names—was murdered."

"What's his name?"

"She wouldn't tell. She said he was married and devoted to his children and had a jealous wife. If the guy's wife knew he'd been working with her she'd divorce him and Beverly would be blackballed in her profession."

Bernstein, who had been doodling on a scratch-pad, looked up. "I can get a line on the agency that handles the Barker woman. I'll call our fashion editor, who can run it down without trouble. Don't stick your chin out, Heald. If I pass on any information to you, you can give it to the police on your own but I am keeping strictly out until we have a story we can print. Clear?"

"That's a lot more than I should expect," Mike said.

Bernstein grinned. "You're damned right it is. Now get out. I have a newspaper to run." He lighted a fresh cigarette and shook his head. "I smoke too many of these things."

II

Mike checked out of the University Club and returned to Forsyth's house late in the afternoon. He reported on his activities and, when he saw Forsyth's alarm, he said quickly, "Bernstein is as straight as they come. He won't print until we give him the high sign. And he's trying to run down Beverly Barker's alibi for me."

"I wish to God you and Jane would sit back and leave this to the police and Ralph Cummins. Look what's already happened to Jane!"

"How is Jane?"

"She's been sleeping ever since she got home. Her bodyguard is in her sitting room mending a black lace evening dress."

"A what?"

Forsyth smiled. "I was surprised too. But she says when she goes out in the evening with her husband—he's a fireman and they aren't often off together—she likes to dress up and feel feminine."

Mike shook his head. "Women!"

At his tone of disillusionment Forsyth's lips twitched.

"The man of experience," he murmured, and Mike grinned.

Forsyth reached out to silence his telephone, spoke, and then said, "He's right here," and held it out to Mike.

"This is Heald."

"Bernstein. Got something for you but damned if I know what it means. Just confuses things. Beverly Barker didn't have an agent. She worked only for the Biltmore Fashion Mart, modeling evening clothes and occasionally working for charity benefits, now and then displaying furs on the main floor, but mostly she modeled for salesmen when they came in twice a year to look at the new lines. The Biltmore has its own designers. She must be pretty good because her boss was talking of sending her to Paris openings next season. He's the general manager of the Mart, guy named Filton, Horace Filton. Well known in the trade. Man already high up the ladder and headed for bigger and better things. And the night of the murder he was playing poker with a group of six men. Incidentally he never had any children—to his knowledge— and he is now married to his third wife and the marriage is breaking up. He wants out. So the jealous wife stuff is for the birds."

"In other words," Mike said in a tone of satisfaction, "Beverly Barker hasn't the shadow of an alibi."

"That's the way it looks. And see here, Heald, has it occurred to you—I'll bet it has to the police—that there are now two sets of alibis to check?"

"What do you mean?"

"Whoever kidnaped Jane Forsyth this morning must have to account for that time somehow."

"It gets more and more tangled."

"Tell the police about the Barker angle but leave out the *Chronicle* if you can."

"Thank you," Mike said.

He ran down Detective Forman with some difficulty and when he identified himself he was greeted with something less than delight.

"You!"

"Me," Mike agreed cheerfully.

"Don't tell me you've lost your cousin again."

"No, I've run down an alibi for you and blown it sky-high."

"Look." Forman sounded as though he were on the verge of bursting into tears. "Don't you learn anything? Look what happened—what nearly happened—to Miss Forsyth. Keep out! I don't want to have to tell you again."

"If you'll just listen," Mike said, and Forman gave a loud, martyred sigh. "Beverly Barker doesn't have an agent. She works for one outfit, the Biltmore Fashion Mart. You know that big store on Fifth Avenue and they sell their special designs all around the country. Biltmore, apparently, carries a big punch like Dior. Beverly's boss was playing poker on the night of the murder. Incidentally he has no children and he is divorcing his third wife, so the jealous wife angle is out."

"Well," Forman said, "who would have believed that Heald had his uses? So now rest on your laurels, will you not, and we'll carry on from here."

"What about the kid, the one with the harelip? Jane will be worrying about him."

"He's being checked out. He lives with foster parents who don't seem interested in anything but the money they collect for his keep. The gang he mentioned is a pain in the neck to the police and it would help if this guy could give us some names, something to work on and get our teeth into. They go through a neighborhood like Grant taking Richmond. Guilty of everything so far but murder and rape. This boy is head of his high school class but a social outcast. Kids that age are cruel little beasts. Make his life miserable."

Forman added politely, "If there is anything else I can tell you, don't hesitate to ask. My time, as the crooner used to sing, is your time."

Mike found himself laughing. He couldn't help liking Forman. "Well, since you are so obliging, did you check on Toyman's alibi?"

"And why Toyman, for God's sake? He was going to set Lawrence up for life."

"Well, he's the only man to surface so far in this deal."

"If," Forman said with studied control, "You can imagine Toyman shacking up at a motel with Lawrence—"

Mike let out a shout of laughter. "Look, man," he said when he was serious again, "come on and give."

"Why I listen to your blandishments I don't know." Forman was resigned. "Toyman went to that convention of toymakers on Friday, just as he said he did. Wowed them. He had the star attractions, apparently, with orders pouring in. Mobbed by potential buyers."

"But Thursday night?"

"He had an abscessed tooth. People at the convention on Friday said he looked drawn and sick, but he would after an ordeal like that. Leaves poison in the system. Happened to my wife once. Wasn't like herself for a week."

"Did you check on the dentist?"

"Okay," Forman said, speaking to someone else. He turned back to the telephone. "I'd be delighted to chat with you all day or dance all night or whatever, except that I have work to do. But don't hesitate to interrupt me if you come up with any more ideas." He broke the connection.

When Mike had repeated the gist of the conversation to Forsyth, the latter said thoughtfully, "You know, Mike, we've got to be on the wrong track. The only people we've unearthed were all at the funeral service this afternoon. So how could any of them have abducted Jane?"

"But Jane was there too," Mike pointed out. He added, "If the murderer was there, it must have been a shock to see Jane walk in."

After a long pause Forsyth said, "Hank Fitch's widow was there. The one with the dark glasses."

14

THE POLICEWOMAN looked up approvingly as Jane came into the sitting room. She put aside the black lace dress, folding it neatly.

"That rest did you good. Heaven knows you needed it. What with one thing and another."

"Murder and kidnaping and then that ghastly funeral," Jane said. "And a week ago everything seemed all serene. I feel as though I had been tossed in the air on a blanket, only I can't get my feet down on solid ground."

"You will. And now," Mrs. Talent said briskly, "let's get the situation clear. Your butler or whatever you call him has been checked out by the police. Good war record, been with your uncle for the past fifteen years, no trouble before that. A good shot. He's been issued a revolver."

Jane was startled. "Surely that isn't necessary. It sounds as though this house was in a state of siege."

The policewoman ignored this. "There's a tap on the telephones here." She added quickly, "With Mr. Forsyth's knowledge and consent. If you get any suspicious calls, try to keep whoever it is talking as long as possible. With dial phones it takes time to check a call. No one is to be admitted to the house unless he or she is personally known to you and with your consent. You are not to leave, for any reason, without me. I think that about covers it."

"Yes, I guess it does. How long is this to go on?"

"Until we get hold of that joker."

"And if you don't—"

"Sometimes a murder can be a result of a quarrel over twenty-five cents. Kids have killed their parents over something like that. Or the work of maniacs. But a murder followed by an attempt to kill you to stop you interfering—no, sister. There's motive somewhere."

"If we could establish just one alibi that would hold up—"

"Find the motive and you can break down any alibi. So what makes you dangerous to someone?"

Jane shook her head. "I wish I knew."

"I can't figure why the kidnaper left the keys in that old car."

"He or she didn't expect me to be found. Not in the trunk and with the garage door closed and the street almost empty and the house deserted. No one had lived there for a long time."

"How do you know that?" Hilda Talent said sharply.

"Why he—the voice—said so."

The policewoman got up. "It's a wonder to me you didn't tell us that in the first place."

"Why?"

"Because it means the kidnaper knew the owner of that house. The car is registered to a man named Giddings. Sam Giddings. He used to live there but moved out a couple of years ago. The police are looking for him now."

"Giddings?" Jane shook her head. "I never heard of him."

"I'll call in to report. Anything else you remember?" Mrs. Talent picked up Jane's telephone, jabbed the numbers with a thick forefinger, and identified herself. "Sure, she's okay. Right here with me. She just remembered that the person who kidnaped her said the house had been unoccupied for a long time and no one was likely to come... Well, she didn't see the significance, of course. . . . No calls. No visitors."

Dinner was a quiet affair that night. The presence of the policewoman checked any personal conversation and they were all too upset to be able to indulge in small talk. Hilda Talent chewed her way calmly through her dinner, taking quick appraising glances around her, waiting to see which fork Jane used, and observing the way in which she helped herself as the dishes were served. She was a quick learner and made no mistakes. Nor did she make any effort to break through the uneasy silence.

After dinner Forsyth showed her the small television room between the drawing room and his bookroom and she settled down contentedly, much to Jane's relief.

"We don't have to be Siamese twins," the policewoman said. "Just don't answer the door or go out without me." She turned dials, found a comedian, and watched, laughing heartily from time to time.

For a while Jane sat with her uncle and Mike in the bookroom and then she got up. "I'm tired. I don't know why because I slept two hours this afternoon, but—"

"Go to bed," Forsyth advised her, "and don't worry. Your bodyguard will have the twin bed in your room, between you and the door. Good night, my dear." Then he came to put his arm around her and hold her close. "Thank God you are all right and under your own roof again. Safe." Then he released her. "Happy dreams."

It was long after she had left them that Forsyth said, "But this can't go on indefinitely. Sooner or later, something has to break. This guy Giddings—that's a new complication."

"But if he was involved, the last place he'd leave Jane would be in his own car in his own garage."

"But he knows the killer. If the killer knows about his house, about his car—"

Forsyth answered the telephone. "Yes, this is James Forsyth... *Who!*" It was almost a shout and the policewoman appeared in the doorway, alert, watchful. Forsyth gestured for her to get to another telephone and check the call. She ran for the nearest phone in the kitchen.

"Yes," Forsyth said, "yes, Mr. Giddings." And Mike leaped out of his chair. "The police... what?... found you where? Yonkers?... Yes, your car was involved in a kidnaping and attempted murder... My niece... Of course I'll talk to you. Can you come here? Okay, I'll wait all night if necessary."

He put down the telephone and Mike said, "You mean this guy Giddings has really showed up?"

"And very much put out. Says the police traced him to his present address in Yonkers, where he's been living for a year and a half. He has a job selling tires and rents a room across the street from the shop. His house has been on the market for about two years, but no takers because it needs a good deal of work: plumbing inadequate, furnace broken down, leaking roof. And he deliberately left his old car with the keys in it, hoping it would be stolen and he'd be able to collect insurance. He doesn't know anything about any kidnaping—he says—and he's on his way down here now."

"Do you think he'll get here?" Mike asked.

The policewoman had come in so quietly that they were not aware of her presence until she said, "He'll get here. He'll have a police escort. They traced the call. He was in Yonkers as he said and they'll see he is delivered." She had brought with her a big handbag holding a businesslike revolver. "I just checked on Miss Forsyth. She's sound asleep. Partly shock, partly a kind of escape from all she's been through, not just the discomfort and the terror of not knowing what might happen."

The time seemed endless. Actually it was only three-quarters of an hour before the quiet was disturbed by the roar of a motorcycle, which came to a stop outside the house. A grim-faced Johnson, hand in his pocket, went to open the door. Outside a police car slowed down and then moved away.

Sam Giddings was young, about twenty-five, big, broad-shouldered, light on his feet, with a broken nose and neglected teeth. At first glance a plug-ugly. At second glance a very worried young man.

"You Mr. Forsyth?"

"Sit down, Giddings. My nephew, Michael Heald. Mrs. Talent."

"Will you, for God's sake, tell me what this is all about? Kidnaping and murder, for Chrissake!" Giddings mopped his head with a handkerchief that was not overclean. "Using my car—and this dame—" He looked at Mrs. Talent.

"No, it was my niece, Miss Forsyth, who was kidnaped."

"But why me? Why do the cops want me? I've never laid eyes on the girl. I swear to God I never have."

It was the policewoman who said, "She got a fake telephone call this morning, saying the caller knew who had killed the guy she thought she was married to. She went to a movie theater in the Bronx to meet him, she was knocked out by some drug, and she came to in the trunk of your car in your garage. The kidnaper said not to expect any help because the house had been empty a long time."

"So?" He was belligerent.

"So," the policewoman said calmly, "who knew it had been empty a long time?"

Both Mike and Forsyth were content to let Hilda Talent take over the questioning.

"Anyone in the neighborhood, I suppose: the real estate people, the—how the hell would I know?"

"And the car with the keys in it?"

He grinned. "It wasn't worth twenty-five dollars in the

open market, but I thought if someone stole it I could collect insurance. But no one was dumb enough to do it."

"So someone just accidentally knew about the vacant house and the convenient car."

"I suppose so. Gosh, how would I know? I keep my nose clean. Only one count against me, drunk and disorderly. And that was three years ago!"

"How long since you've driven your car?"

"Over a year."

"And the battery started right up?"

Giddings was perspiring. "I don't understand this any more than you do."

"If you couldn't sell your house, did you ever rent it or lend it to anyone? Let anyone stay there?"

"Why, I—" His mouth fell open. "Sure, I turned it over to a pal of mine for a few weeks when he was down and out. It was summer and Charlie didn't care that the furnace didn't work and all that."

"Charlie?"

"Charles Lawrence. We've lost touch but we knew each other quite well for a while."

They had met in a bar, got jawing the way you do after a couple of beers, went to a hamburg joint for supper. They were both on the loose. Picked up a couple of girls. Met now and then. Once Charlie had been dead broke and he'd let him stay at the house he had abandoned. Once Charlie was flush and gave Sam a couple of twenties. Seemed to be well heeled at the time.

"When was this?"

"Back a couple of years ago, before the broke time."

"When did you see him last?"

"Well, I got this job in Yonkers, a nice steady job and a chance to move up to head salesman. Retirement and sick-leave and fringe benefits. You know. Worth sticking it out.

Then Charlie got some job as a salesman in New Jersey or working out of New Jersey. Last time I saw him was a month or six weeks ago. Ran into him in a bar on Irving Place. We lifted a few and he said he was on to a good thing. Fine future. Everything all saucer and blowed. He was heading right for the top."

"Was he the kind to boast or was it for real?" the policewoman asked.

"Well, he boasted. But this time it was for real. He had that cocky turn to his head he got when he was really on top of things. Said he was married. When I asked who the lucky girl was, he laughed and said, 'You pays your money and you takes your choice.' Always joking, you know. Anything for a laugh with Charlie."

Mike's face was bloodless and the policewoman gave him a shrewd look. A volcano. That's what the guy was, a volcano.

"Did he tell you how to reach him?" Forsyth asked.

"He said he was selling kids' toys, but I thought that was a gag. Said he expected to go into partnership within a year and after that he'd be coming into the big money. I don't know how you could find him—"

"Oh, we know where he is," the policewoman said. "He was cremated this morning. Murdered last Thursday night or early Friday morning at the Regal Motel on Manhattan."

"Charlie! God! Not Charlie!" Giddings mopped his face again.

"How did you miss the story? Front page in the papers and on television with his picture."

"I turned my television in on a color set and it hasn't been delivered yet. Waiting until I move into the apartment I've taken. And I don't often see a paper." Giddings looked from face to face. "Charlie! My God."

Forsyth rang for drinks. "What's yours?"

"Beer, if you have it. After getting arrested that time I've laid off the hard stuff."

Forsyth raised his brows and Johnson nodded. In a few minutes he returned with a tray, glasses, whiskey, a siphon, and an opened bottle of beer with a pewter mug.

"Well," Giddings raised the mug after filling it carefully, "here's how." He drank in long thirsty gulps and set down the empty mug. "I needed that. Getting it right between the eyes without warning, about someone you've palled around with and saw just a few weeks ago on top of the world."

He was silent and the two men waited. At last he said, "You know, it just doesn't seem possible, unless—it was a motel, you say?—some woman—Charlie always had a way with women. I've got a steady girl now and we're talking about getting married next month. She's got a job as a hairdresser near my shop. The time comes when a guy ought to stop horsing around and settle down, but Charlie had a saying that there was only one way to deal with women: use them and leave them."

"Mike!" Forsyth said, the word like an explosion, and the younger man settled back in his chair.

"Well, if that's all," Giddings got awkwardly out of his chair. He was one of those people who do not know how to take leave gracefully. He hovered. "If there is anything else—"

"We'd like your address and telephone number and the name of your boss," the policewoman said.

"I gave all that to the Yonkers police. Say, you won't make me any trouble with my boss, will you? Stella and I are all set—"

"Speaking of trouble," Forsyth broke in hastily, "I want to pay you for your time and trouble in coming here." He pulled a couple of twenties from his billfold. "We are very grateful to you."

"Well, thanks a lot. Any time. Well, that is—"

"Mr. Giddings will always be available," Mrs. Talent said grimly.

He looked at her. "You on the cops?"

"I'm on the cops."

"Well, like I said, I'm clean." He made an awkward gesture and went out, closely followed by Johnson. The front door closed.

"The police will keep an eye on him and check his story," Mrs. Talent told Mike in a tone of reassurance.

Mike gave a short laugh. "Only one human being knew about that empty house and the car with keys in it, and he's dead!"

15

THE HAND came over Jane's mouth and she felt the prick of the needle in her arm. She tried to cry out but no sound came from her throat. Through her paralyzing fear dim memories struggled. Someone was lifting her out of her seat, someone's arm was around her, supporting her stumbling feet out of the dank theater onto the street. But this wasn't the way she had come in. This was a side exit. She was helped into the front seat of a car, her head fell back and she slept.

The rest was hard to remember. There was the squeak of a rusty garage door being forced open and then she was dragged out of the car.

A gag was tied so that she could make no sound and her eyes were too heavy to lift. Then her hands were jerked behind her back and bound, the strain pulling at her upper arms and shoulders. She was lifted and pushed into the trunk of another car. Her eyes were open now but she was turned away from her abductor. It did not occur to her to struggle. Her most immediate problem was a surge of acute nausea, which she had to fight. It swept over her, wave after wave, and she tried to control it by sheer will power.

And all the time she was aware of the whispering voice telling her that she was in the trunk of an abandoned car in the garage of an abandoned house. She'd never get out. Never. Then the trunk lid slammed down and she heard the creak of the garage door closing.

She moaned, tossing from side to side, and the anxious policewoman got up and switched on the light. The girl was either delirious or in the throes of a nightmare. She touched her skin and was relieved. She wasn't feverish, just struggling with some chimeras of her own tortured mind. Well, it was small wonder, poor kid. She'd taken a lot of blows and taken them well. This was the first sign of breaking.

Jane moaned, recalling the tire iron on which she had lain. Her legs stirred as she relived her attempts to kick on the trunk lid, to raise an alarm. But there was no sound at all as her bare feet touched the soft bedding.

Mike! she cried, but no sound came out. Mike! Something terrible was happening to her and she did not know why. And then suddenly she did know, know clearly who was doing this to her. And that was impossible.

Then she heard the protesting sound as the garage door opened, and the vibration as the motor caught. The car was moving now, jolted over a curb, headed into traffic. Going where? No one could have found her in the garage. Then why was she being moved? Where was she being taken?

She was in heavy traffic. She could hear the throbbing of truck motors, the horns of impatient motorists, the scream of brakes as a careless driver was caught by a light.

After what seemed to be hours there was no sound of traffic and the car stopped. In the silence she summoned all her strength and kicked against the trunk lid. It didn't make much sound but she repeated it until once more she had to stop, exhausted by the lack of air.

The trunk was opened and she was turned over, half blinded by the light, and looked into a stranger's disfigured face. There were fingers on her wrist and she screamed.

She opened her eyes and saw the policewoman standing beside her bed, a fantastic figure in striped pajamas that made her look like a beach umbrella, fingers on her wrist.

"It's all right," Mrs. Talent said calmly. "You've just had a bad dream. Your heart is pounding. I'm going down to heat some milk for you. You'll be all right. I'll lock you in."

"I'm sorry. I dreamed—I remembered everything—and I knew who had done it, who had abducted me, who wanted me to die."

"Who?"

Jane shook her head. "It's gone now. It's all gone."

"It will come back." The policewoman went to the door of the sitting room. "Who is it?"

"What's going on?" Mike called. "I heard a scream."

"Miss Forsyth had a nightmare but she's all right now. I'm going to lock her in while I fix her some hot milk."

"I'll stay with her."

"No one stays with her," Mrs. Talent said curtly. "That's an order, mister."

"You can't believe I'd hurt Jane! For God's sake, what reason—"

"Well, for one thing," said Mrs. Talent, who didn't believe a word of it, "we've found out that Mr. Forsyth has drawn up a will dividing his estate between the two of you. It's quite a pile. And if one of you is eliminated, winner takes all."

"But I don't need it!"

"I've yet to hear of anyone who thought he had enough. Go back to bed, Mr. Heald. Now see what you've done," she added in disgust as Forsyth came out of his room, tying a dressing gown around him, hair rumpled.

"What's wrong?" he asked, startled.

"Just Mr. Heald raising a rumpus. Send him back to bed. Miss Forsyth had a bad dream and I'm going down to heat her some milk." She closed and locked the sitting-room door and dropped the key in her pocket with a challenging look at the two men. With a muttered oath Mike swung around and went back to his own room.

The policewoman looked after him thoughtfully. "Nasty temper that young man has."

"I suppose," Forsyth said, "she will continue to need a guard."

"She needs a guard," Mrs. Talent said grimly.

"Exactly what are you afraid of?"

"When she had that nightmare tonight, she remembered, or thinks she remembered, who was behind her abduction. She's forgotten it now, but the knowledge is there and that makes her dangerous, Mr. Forsyth. I'm explaining this to you because you have a right to know, but I don't want anyone else to know she has that dangerous memory buried in her subconscious. No one."

"If you think Mike—"

"Mr. Heald is not to be told."

"But—" Forsyth stared at her. Then he shook his head. "Oh, nonsense! Just because the boy has a temper—"

"Mr. Heald is not to be told," she repeated.

"All right," he conceded, "but you are wrong, you know. I'd stake my life on Mike."

"What about your niece's life?" Without waiting for a reply she unlocked the door of Jane's sitting room and went in, closing and locking it behind her. She stood holding the glass of hot milk and looked down at Jane, who had already fallen into a deep sleep.

II

It was nearly noon when Jane awakened. She still felt tired and unrefreshed. Her body was bruised and lame from being trapped in the trunk. There were hollows under the eyes that looked too big for her face, her mouth twitched. When Mrs. Talent turned on the bathroom tap, she gave a nervous start.

Hilda came back with a damp washcloth, wiped her face

and hands, brushed her hair, and propped pillows behind her.

"You're to stay in bed all day. Doctor's orders."

Jane nodded. "That's all right with me. I feel as though I'd never be able to move again, as though I'd been beaten black and blue."

"You'll feel better after you've eaten. I've called down for your breakfast."

"I'm hungry," Jane announced in surprise.

The policewoman admitted Johnson, set up the folding table across Jane's lap, and watched while Johnson put down the tray.

"Good morning." Jane tried to speak cheerfully, though her voice was a kind of croak.

"Good morning, Miss Forsyth. My wife made you one of your favorite omelets. It will just melt in your mouth, and some corn muffins. There's cantaloupe and a pot of coffee. If you want anything else—"

"Thank her for me," Jane said, and the policewoman ushered Johnson out, exchanged grim looks with him, and locked the door.

When she had devoured her breakfast and drained a second cup of coffee, there was a little color in Jane's face, though her eyes were still shadowed and her mouth twitched with nerves.

"Nothing like food, is there?" the policewoman said cheerfully. "Later I'll give you a sponge bath and fix you up a bit, but you might as well rest for a few minutes first." She bustled around the room and paused in front of the dressing table mirror where she could watch Jane's face. "Do you remember that nightmare you had?" she asked casually.

Jane shivered. "I was scared," she admitted. "Scared silly. And awfully sick. More than anything I remember trying not to be sick."

"Don't force it. It will probably come back, bit by bit."

"I'd rather forget it."

"No doubt. But the more you can remember, the more it will help us find this joker and put him out of business. Then you can leave the whole thing behind you and there won't be any more nightmares."

"Yes, I see. I remember one thing. I wasn't taken out of the theater the way I came in; we went out through a side door marked Fire Exit." Unobtrusively the policewoman dug a notebook and pencil out of her capacious handbag, in which the revolver gleamed, and made notes.

"I was moved from one car to another. I'd been in the front seat of the first car and then I was dumped in the trunk of the other. I was gagged and my hands were tied behind my back." She moved painful shoulders.

"After your bath I'll give you a nice massage and relieve some of those sore muscles."

"The whispering voice said the house was unoccupied and no one would ever find me in the car. It had been there a long time. Only—" she paused, frowning. "Would an old car start like that, right away? This one did."

"Someone had put in a new battery. The police have found out a lot. The car belonged to a guy named Sam Giddings." She watched Jane's face.

"Giddings? Who is he and why would he kidnap me?"

"He seems to be in the clear. They ran him down through his license plates. And that, I think, is where this joker slipped up. He had foresight enough to put in a new battery, but he never thought about the license plates. It just takes one slip."

Mrs. Talent described the tracing of the ownership of the car to Sam Giddings and how he had come to the house the night before, baffled and scared half out of his wits at being involved in murder and kidnaping.

"But what possible connection did he have with me?"

"He had an old pal named Charlie Lawrence to whom he turned the house over once when this Lawrence was broke."

"Chris! But this makes no sense at all."

"It will."

Jane abandoned the puzzle. "What about Stan Wiltshire?"

"He's okay. The police have been checking him out. So far so good. They've talked to the foster parents who can't stand him but are glad to get the money the state pays them for his keep. And the kid is cooperating with the police, telling them all he knows about the gang, their names, their actions, their hideouts, where they get marijuana, the works. They are being picked up all over the place."

"They won't hurt Stan?" Jane asked in quick alarm.

"The police have him in protective custody. They intend to turn him over to Mr. Forsyth, who will do what he can for the boy. Apparently he owes him a lot."

"I'm glad. Oh, I'm so glad. If you can get a message to him, will you say 'thank you' for me?"

"He'll get the message."

Fortified by breakfast, Jane insisted that she could manage a tub bath and when Mrs. Talent had worked on her sore shoulders and brushed her hair, which her arms were too lame to do, and helped her into a light robe, Jane asked to be allowed to lie on the chaise longue in her sitting room. The policewoman agreed. While Jane turned over the pages of a book without understanding a word she read, Mrs. Talent sat back contentedly to watch daytime television on Jane's small screen.

"It isn't often I get a chance to do this. When I retire, I'm going to watch soap operas all afternoon every single day. And I'll get a really good color set. It just isn't the same on black and white."

Jane held the book as a kind of protection, after explaining to the policewoman that she could use an ear plug for the set. She was trying to recapture the moment of enlightenment when she had learned the reason for Chris's death and the attempt to kill her. But there was only fog where there had been that revealing flash of light.

Instead she thought about Chris. She could do that now. Look at him steadily, accept the fact of his murder, come to terms with the knowledge of the stranger with whom she had lived for a year.

All those absences when he had been with another woman or other women. The money he had obtained somehow, while she had struggled to make a home out of that dark basement apartment. Disloyal? Yes. Probably he had married her in the expectation of getting her money. That too. But he had taught her to love. He had made her happy. She had learned laughter and gaiety and lightness of heart from him. Whatever he had been, she couldn't hate him. She couldn't forget him. She would remember always that, mistaken or not, she had loved him. And the knowledge brought her a curious sense of peace that now a page of her life could be turned without bitterness and she could look forward with courage to what lay ahead.

The ringing of her telephone startled her but did not arouse the policewoman absorbed in the fictitious drama she was watching, particularly as, at that moment, the telephone on the screen rang too.

It was the whispering voice again and Jane waved frantically to the policewoman, who grasped the situation and ran downstairs for another phone.

"I was just checking up, my dear. You were lucky this time. Mind your own business and you might stay lucky. Keep your cousin out of trouble. You wouldn't like him to get hurt, would you? I thought not." There was a sound like smothered laughter.

16

THE Baltimore Fashion Mart was one of the most flourishing institutions in the garment trade. It had long since discarded any attempt at the middle-class trade and it was now determined to rival Saks Fifth Avenue, I. Magnin, and the other great houses, carrying its name the length and breadth of the country. A Biltmore dress might be an expensive luxury, but its status value was incalculable.

Mike, who had never taken any interest in women's clothes, noticed in passing that the great windows on Fifth Avenue each held a single dress with its accessories. To his untrained eyes they seemed to be simply cut, but the colors were pleasing and women hovered, exclaiming.

The first floor was carpeted and the air was scented with a light fragrance created for Biltmore. The clerks wore simple black dresses and spoke in muted voices to their clients, whom they addressed as madam and not, as in cheaper stores, as dear.

An elevator, its walls lined with mirrors, took Mike to the sixth floor where he was asked to wait while a clerk went the length of the block-long building, passing models in unlikely poses, wearing extravagant negligees. One of these creations draped on a six-foot-high figure of emaciated dimensions was being examined by two women in their middle forties, both buxom.

"Three hundred and fifty dollars!" one of them exclaimed. "That's a lot of money."

"Well, dear, face it," said the other. "At our ages the upkeep gets more expensive."

The clerk came hurrying back. "Mr. Tilson will see you for ten minutes. This way." She led him back to an office whose door she opened. A pretty girl looked up from her typewriter. "Mr. Heald? Mr. Tilson will see you."

With the air of one ushering a subject into the presence of a monarch, she flung open an inner door. The office was immense, with all the appurtenances necessary to a prestige setting: wall-to-wall carpeting, heavy draperies cunningly folded to reveal glimpses of Fifth Avenue, soundless because of air-conditioning. A smooth, tall, attractive man of forty, who had kept his weight down by exercise, and whose face was bronzed by tropical suns or a sunlamp, rose to greet him, standing behind a huge shining desk that held nothing but an onyx pen and pencil set, a Steuben ashtray, and an intercom, as well as a couple of telephones, whose color matched the draperies.

"Mr. Heald?" He held out a well-groomed hand, waved to a deep leather chair beside the desk.

"This is quite a setup," Mike commented as he seated himself.

Tilson frowned. He could enjoy a laugh as well as the next man, but his status was not a subject for amusement. It had required too long and too tough a climb.

"You wanted to see me?" He glanced at his watch.

"Yes. There seems to be some question about Beverly Barker's alibi for the time when Charles Lawrence was murdered. He, if you recall, presumably was married to her."

Tilson scraped back his chair. "You from the cops?" Some of his carefully cultivated accent dropped away and he sounded more like the young man who had clawed his way to this position and was prepared to fight for it.

"No, I'm a cousin of the other girl whom Lawrence married."

"So?"

"Beverly Barker claims to have an alibi for the night of the murder. You seem to be the alibi."

"Look, I've told the police what I know about this thing. I'm sorry for your cousin but, damn it, all that concerns me is running this business. I don't want to get involved in murder. And I was not—get this, *not*—with Beverly that night. I was playing poker and I can bring some men from my club to vouch for it. And they weren't all my friends; a couple of them were just men I'd seen around, the way you do. No reason to back my story if it weren't true. And they'd remember that game because I was the heavy loser. Went down three thousand dollars. So that covers this business of being Beverly's alibi. And, I repeat, I don't want to get involved in murder. I've given you your ten minutes—"

Mike did not budge. As Forman could have told the annoyed store manager, the young man was not easily sidetracked. "It's murder and kidnaping now," he said, and Tilson sank back in his chair. "Yesterday morning my cousin was kidnaped and only by the wildest fluke was she discovered in time to save her life."

"You don't think I kidnaped this cousin of yours? For God's sake, man, why would I?"

Mike grinned. "I'm interested in you only in so far as you are involved with Beverly Barker."

"Well, what do you want to know?"

"Where was she yesterday? Did she report for work as usual?"

Tilson spoke on the intercom to his secretary and the voice came through clearly. "Just a minute, Mr. Tilson

... Oh, here it is. She had the day off to attend her husband's funeral. In fact, she asked for several days off. She's been modeling the fall line of furs and she was exhausted. Of course there was no question of refusing."

"Of course not." Tilson switched off the intercom. "Well?"

"What do you know about this girl?"

"She's a fine model, a natural, one of the best we've ever had. Got the figure for it. She can make anything look good."

"Does she work for you full time?"

"She works for the Mart full time," Tilson corrected. "She does some modeling here in the store, fall and spring showings, and occasionally some smart dress or suit or coat down on the main floor, but a big part of her work is displaying our new designs for our out-of-town outlets. She wows them. In fact, I was thinking of sending her to Paris for the new showings there. She's got flair and clothes sense and a real future—if she keeps out of trouble. Well, you might guess for yourself if you've ever seen her."

"I saw her at the funeral when she couldn't have been nastier to my cousin."

"What do you expect when you get a couple of rival women together? Ask me, brother. I'm an authority. I'm taking off time next month to go to Reno to divorce my third. I've spent the past five months scraping her off barroom floors. Every time the telephone rings I think it is someone calling me to come and collect her. God, what a life! No more domestic bliss for me. From now on I play the field. Three wives is three too many."

"And Beverly?" Mike asked with the persistence of a dripping tap.

"Look, I told you. She's a good model. One of the best. I wouldn't like to lose her. But if she's mixed up in murder and kidnaping, I want no part of her. The Mart wants no part of her. Mars the image. Is that clear? I have no personal interest in Beverly Barker."

"How is she on the tiles?"

"How the hell would I know?" Then Tilson grinned reluctantly. "Okay, a couple of little incidents. Nothing serious. And that was before she got married, or so I thought. I wouldn't kill any guy to get her."

"Would she kill a guy to get you?"

For a moment Tilson preened himself and then selfpreservation took over. "I never promise marriage unless I mean it," he said virtuously. "And, like I said, three times and out."

"Well, if she wasn't shacked up with you and she wasn't the woman at the motel, where was she?"

"That's your problem, mister. And now I've got a store to run." Tilson answered the intercom. "Yes, right away. And tell him to bring his sketches for those new window displays."

II

Armed with the Irving Place address, furnished by Tilson's secretary, Mike hailed a cab. This one wasn't air-conditioned.

"Going to be another scorcher," the cabbie said cheerfully. "Say it will be up to ninety by afternoon. Feels like it now."

Beverly Barker, wearing a bikini, was sitting under a fan removing polish from her nails. The door was open for ventilation.

"Miss Barker?" Mike took a long pleased look at her. "I am Michael Heald. I'm not selling anything." He had an engaging smile. "But if you would give me a few minutes—"

She gave him a close scrutiny, nodded, and took her time slipping into a light robe. She settled down on the couch, waving to a seat beside her.

Like the policemen before him, Mike found it more prudent to take a chair facing her.

"And what might you want?" she asked.

"I've come to ask you for a couple of alibis."

"Why, you—you aren't even on the cops. I can smell them at ten yards. What are you, a reporter?" She hesitated, obviously evaluating the possible value of any publicity he might give her. Then she recognized him. "Oh, you're little Jane's faithful watchdog! You can get the hell out of here and, if you're smart, you'll mind the store and leave this to someone else."

"Is that a warning?" he asked softly.

"You're damned right that's a warning." She reached for a small squat stone vase on the table that held artificial flowers. He caught her arm and for a moment they struggled for possession of the vase she had intended to use as a weapon. Then unexpectedly—or, he thought, inevitably—she relaxed, her body pressing against his.

Okay, he thought wearily, we'll play it her way. He kissed her, the overrouged, sticky mouth clinging to his. She let the robe fall open and slid down on the couch, pulling him down beside her.

Mike reached for a cigarette with fingers that trembled a little. "You pack quite a charge," he said mildly.

"So I've been told." She smiled at him.

"Your boss thinks you're hot stuff."

Her eyes narrowed. "You've seen Tilson?"

"I've just come from him."

"Why?"

"I wanted to know where you were on a couple of occasions. Like yesterday, for example. I understand you got a few days off."

"Yesterday I went to my husband's funeral. And they

owed me some extra time. Modeling furs in this heat! And having to do it over and over because the sweat showed up on my face. What do they expect, for God's sake!"

"I wouldn't know. The thing is that you don't have an agent who worked with you the night Lawrence was bumped off. Your boss was playing poker. So where were you and what were you doing?"

"I didn't kill Chester. I was crazy about him, if you want to know. Just nuts. So why would I? I didn't know about Baby Jane. But someone seems to think—Look, this room was just about torn apart by someone searching it. What were they looking for?"

"At a guess a wallet stuffed with hundred-dollar bills."

"Chester! You've got to be kidding."

"He was loaded when he checked in at that motel. When he was found, the wallet was gone and so was the money."

Beverly was deep in thought, no longer interested in any sex play. She was, above all, practical.

"Chester wasn't making much. Well, look at this pad! But he had it made for the future. He wasn't lying about that. He was on to something good. But meantime it took most of what he made to keep up a good impression, nice clothes, money for entertainment. Things like that are necessary for a salesman."

Mike stood up to crush out his cigarette and took advantage of the movement to regain his former seat on the chair facing the couch. Beverly seemed unaware of the maneuver. She was frowning, deep in thought.

"Where were you yesterday morning before the funeral?"

"Buying that widow's veil."

"Can you prove that?"

"What gives, anyhow?"

"My cousin Jane was abducted and only saved by the

sheerest chance, so narrow a chance that I can hardly take it in, even now."

"Well, well." There was a long pause. "Well, well," Beverly repeated thoughtfully. She added inexplicably, "I have a good memory for faces. An excellent memory for faces."

She stood up, tying the robe around her. "On your way, buster. I have work to do."

17

WHILE MIKE was interviewing the manager of the Biltmore Fashion Mart and Beverly Barker, Jane was entertaining another visitor. Mrs. Toyman's ancient Bentley drove up to the curb at the Park Avenue house and she held a long parley at the door with Johnson until he agreed to let her wait inside and went upstairs to confer with Mrs. Talent and Jane.

"Why, of course," Jane said. "I'm terribly sorry you kept her waiting."

The policewoman withdrew to the bedroom but she left the door ajar. "Just a precaution, dear," she said when Jane laughed.

Mrs. Toyman's heavy steps ascended the stairs slowly and then Jane flung open the sitting-room door and went to greet her, hands out. "You shouldn't have come out in all this heat," she said in concern when she had looked at the haggard face. "Do sit here where you'll be comfortable. I understand the temperature has gone up to eighty-five already."

"It's one of those awful days, so muggy. I'm glad you haven't tried to go out."

"I was ordered to spend the day in bed, but I feel better now and I'll sleep more soundly tonight if I don't lie down all day."

"That funeral was too much. I was afraid for you at the time."

"I didn't want to have any service at all," Jane said candidly. "It seemed, after what I had learned about him, that it would just make a Roman holiday for the press."

"It did. I guess you didn't see the papers or hear the news."

"Uncle Jim took care of that."

"Perhaps you shouldn't have gone. Henry and I talked about it but he thought it was only right for Tricks for Tiny Tots to be represented. After all, whatever he turned out to be, Chris had been—" She pressed her handkerchief to her lips.

Jane nodded. "I've thought about it such a lot. Knowing that Chris had another wife—other women—and that our life together had been a lie—it seemed like the end of everything. And then I came to understand that, no matter how much of a dream it was, it had been a happy dream. The man I loved was unreal but the love was real. And that's what counts. I can think of him now and remember the happiness and not be bitter. Grateful for what I had but free of the past."

"How young you are! But I'm glad. I was afraid when you and that nice cousin of yours came to see us on Sunday that you were going to go on digging into the murder, like prodding a sore tooth. I'm glad you are wise enough to let it go. You have so many years ahead of you. You can begin again."

Mrs. Toyman refused Jane's offer of iced coffee, leaning back in her chair, her overweight body sagging a little. She looked around her. "I had no idea you had lived like this before you married Chris. Park Avenue and a butler and—all this." She made a gesture, indicating the room. "Didn't you mind giving it up?"

Jane shook her head.

"Did Chris know about—all this?"

"Yes, he knew. But my uncle, who is also my trustee, refused to let me handle my own money until Chris could prove that he was responsible."

"I wonder why he couldn't be. He had ability, you know. He was a natural salesman."

"Just irresponsible," Jane said. "You look so terribly tired. You must be doing too much in this heat."

"No, the trouble is that I haven't enough to do. I have a cleaning woman once a week and send out the laundry and we eat lightly in hot weather, so time hangs on my hands."

"But Chris," Jane stumbled a little, went on, "Chris told me you were the one who created the toys that have made the business so successful."

"Well, I have a knack that way. Don't know where it came from. My father was a carpenter and my mother brought up nine children in a small town with no labor-saving devices. She had no time for anything beyond housekeeping and cooking and changing diapers and nursing a baby and stretching a small income."

"But you have something really interesting to do, creating things."

"Well, the Christmas line is ready for the market so there's not anything for me to do right now, and I guess I'll have to get used to being idle. Henry has his heart set on retiring and it's high time, of course. He has worked hard all his life and his health isn't any too good. So," there was a long pause, "now Chris is dead, Henry will sell out—he has had a dazzling offer—and we'll move to some warmer place. Henry says El Paso because that's cheap, but I don't know. There's so much to see in southern Europe, but Henry doesn't like to travel. I think if he ever tried it he would enjoy it but then he's a man of set habits and you don't change much at seventy. So things are sort of quiet at home now. That's one reason why I hope you'll come over to New Jersey and stay with us for a while, a few weeks, until—you know —things are straightened out. You wouldn't need a watchdog at the door," and she smiled faintly, "like the one you have now, and you'd be such company for me. You can't imagine! Do come, my dear."

It was hard to meet the pleading eyes and refuse. "I'm afraid they wouldn't let me," Jane said gently. "Right now I'm sort of in a state of siege."

"Why?"

Jane told her about the abduction on the morning of the funeral and her narrow escape.

"Oh, my dear! My dear! A kidnaping on top of everything else."

"It wasn't a kidnaping for ransom. I think someone meant me to die, just as Chris had died, only I don't understand why. I haven't hurt anyone, as Chris did. That other wife, for instance. And there's a woman—old enough to be his mother—how he could! But that is all the past. Only you see I am being guarded until the police find out who wants me dead."

"My dear!" It was a protest.

"I know it sounds rather melodramatic," Jane said apologetically, "but until the one who is doing this is caught—"

"You sound as though it were still going on."

"I got a telephone call in the same whispering voice I heard when I was knocked out in the theater, telling me to mind my own business."

"Isn't there any clue?"

"I don't even know whether it was a man or a woman, just a whispering voice. But whoever did it knew about Sam Giddings' house being empty and about the car he had left there. And only Chris could have known that, because Chris stayed at the house once when he was broke. And Chris is dead. The killer wiped off all the fingerprints in the motel and was careful to remove everything from Chris's pockets, all identification, and took a wallet stuffed with money. Cleaning up like a good housewife."

"Jane, do come to us." Mrs. Toyman was urgent. "You can't live this way. You'd be safe with me. I won't be able to sleep nights if I'm not sure you are all right, and it's not just for your sake. I've got so many hours a day to put in and this may be the last season I do any designing. When Henry sells out, there will be no place for me."

To prevent any return to the discussion of moving to the New Jersey house, Jane said, "Why don't you carry on the business yourself after Mr. Toyman retires? You're the one with the ideas."

Mrs. Toyman shook her head. "I have no business sense at all. I can invent all sorts of cute things, but I wouldn't have any idea how to dispose of them. That's why Henry and I make such a good combination. He has a business head and no imagination. I made my own toys from the time I was a child because we couldn't afford bought ones. And then I began making them for the neighborhood kids."

"How on earth do you get the ideas?"

"I don't know. I see things and imagine other ways of using them, or the ideas just come out of nowhere." Mrs. Toyman looked around and got up to fetch a paperweight that was holding down unanswered letters on Jane's desk. "You could make this so the top would slide open on a hidden hinge and you could use it to hold jewelry. Or," she picked up her handbag and as she jerked its thick handle there was a screaming sound that made Jane leap in her chair.

Mrs. Toyman laughed at herself. "No pickpocket could get away with this. Henry has applied for a patent. It would be useful for women traveling abroad or shopping in crowded stores. It's the only thing I ever thought of as a gadget for adults. You know, in a way, now that the shop will be closing down, I'm just getting warmed up."

She sat, a half smile on her face as she remembered. "I was about twenty and getting awfully tired of helping around the house. I was the oldest kid with the younger ones to look after, especially when my mother's health began to fail. Well, I needed some sort of interest outside the house. There was to be this local fair. So I got together a lot of stuff, just one of a kind, of course, because I didn't have any way of duplicating things, no tools or anything of that sort, and I took a booth at the fair.

"My father thought I was crazy, making children's toys at my age. Well, he'd hardly believe it when I cleaned up. I sold everything I had made and earned more than he did in three months. But it never occurred to me that I could make a business out of doing what I liked best. We sort of grew up thinking that work couldn't be fun. At least, there was something immoral about earning your living at what you do best. Though now I realize it's the best wisdom we ever learn.

"Well, I met Henry at the fair and he was the one who saw the commercial possibilities of the thing. He was a clerk in the local bank, but we didn't do any banking so we had never met. We got going steady, but I didn't think of it like that because he was older than my father. But then we got married and developed this partnership, Tricks for Tiny Tots. That was my name for it and it took on. Of course, the business had to start from scratch, using all Henry's savings and what I'd made at the fair. But from the start it took on and it's a flourishing business now. You'd be surprised to know how it boomed, especially after Chris—"

The spate of words, bottled up for years, seemed to relieve her. She asked hesitantly, "Do you mind? I mean do you mind speaking about Chris?"

"No," Jane assured her. "It's all right now." As the older woman looked at her, she nodded reassuringly. "Honestly it is."

"I sort of envied you two," Mrs. Toyman said. "So young and attractive and romantically in love. Henry and I have had a good partnership but we didn't have all that."

"There were some drawbacks," Jane reminded her dryly.

"I know. I saw that other girl in her widow's weeds. It made me sick to think she'd dare flaunt herself like that, knowing you were the real one. But she is lovely to look at, isn't she? I was never more than passable myself, even as a girl. What is it like, Jane, to be pretty, to have people like just to look at you?"

"Well, I—" Jane fumbled for words. "I'm not all that pretty."

"And you said there was an older woman?"

"Old enough to be his mother. I won't tell you who she is. It's all the past now, anyhow."

"Was it for her money?"

Jane nodded. "Only it wasn't until he—hurt her that she knew that."

"You never really know about people, do you?"

There was a sudden cough and Mrs. Toyman was startled. "I didn't know there was anyone here."

"There's a policewoman guarding me night and day," Jane said, half laughing, half annoyed.

"So you are really safe. Thank God for that!" Mrs. Toyman leaned over to brush her cheek against Jane's. "Keep in touch, my dear. I'm going to be a very lonely woman."

"You go ahead and forge your way on your own. Maybe you don't understand business but you can still make things."

Mrs. Toyman laughed. Then she said, "No, don't get up. I can let myself out."

Apparently this was unnecessary. Johnson was on guard in the front hall and he saw her out of the house and bolted the door behind her.

II

"That looks like the Toymans' old Bentley," Mike remarked as Johnson admitted him.

"A Mrs. Toyman came to see Miss Forsyth. She just left."

Mike ran up the stairs two at a time and tapped at the door of Jane's sitting room. As Mrs. Talent had taken advantage of Mrs. Toyman's departure to stand under a long cool shower in the bathroom she shared with Jane, she was absent from the interview.

"Where have you been?"

"The sleuth twirled his moustache and uttered a hollow laugh."

"Oh, must you be so funny?"

He grinned at her. "Actually I've been on the job." He told her about his interview with the man Tilson at the Mart. "The night Chris was murdered, Beverly wasn't working with her agent, because there is no such animal, and she wasn't with her boss either. He can provide a good solid alibi for the time. He lost his shirt at poker, at least a nice slice of change."

"Beverly Barker?" Jane thought it over. "But I don't see —even suppose she knew about Chris and me—and why go to a motel when they had an apartment? And why try to kill me now that Chris is gone?"

"Because you are so interested in alibis and you advertise the fact in loud, clear terms."

"I'd better be interested," Jane said grimly. "After all, I don't have one myself for Chris's death. And I've got to know who is after me. That whispering voice called again and said you had better keep out if you didn't want to get hurt."

"Well," Mike said in a tone of satisfaction, "business is picking up. Our activities are stirring up some mud."

"It isn't mud we need," she snapped. "It's having things cleared up."

"All in good time, my child. We will now go on to the next chapter of our hero's thrilling adventures." And he described, with some tactful omissions, his interview with Beverly. "And what it all boils down to," he concluded, "is that she hasn't an alibi that is worth a damn. Lying her head off. Just the same—"

"Well?" Jane prodded, as he dropped the subject in a tantalizing manner.

"She knows something," he said soberly. "She said something about being able to recognize faces. I could almost see her thoughts go round while she worked out some plan. If that gal's not up to dirty tricks, I'll eat my hat."

"No, Mike! Don't go on with this. Leave it to the police. That voice—I don't want you hurt. I couldn't bear it if you were hurt."

Suddenly she was in his arms, shivering, clinging to him.

For a moment he held her crushed to him. Then he pushed her away. "Look, kid," he said unsteadily, "brotherly affection is the rot. I'm not even a cousin. And, damn it, I'm not made of stone. Keep away from me."

"Mike?" she said in wonder. "Mike?" It was a cry of incredulous surprise. "I didn't know. Mike!"

This time he did not let her go.

18

THAT NIGHT as they gathered for cocktails and Jane had her usual sherry, Forsyth looked from Jane to Mike and smiled faintly. This was what he had foreseen, had hoped for, ever since he had taken the two young people dearest to him into his home. With Jane's marriage to Chris he had abandoned his plan, but apparently Jane was prepared to live and love again. Chris had done her no permanent damage; he had not even embittered her. At that moment Forsyth felt almost a kind of benevolence for the man he had most disliked.

He was aware, however, of how dangerous this blossoming new love could prove for Mike. In the eyes of the police it would make him an obvious suspect, the person with the strongest motive for eliminating a rival.

One thing sure, he told himself. No one is going to believe that Mike has any financial interest involved. He has about thirty-five thousand a year from his father's estate and when my sister died, after her second marriage, she bequeathed Mike his stepfather's estate, which will bring in double that amount before he is thirty. And Mike is not greatly interested in money. His aim in life is to work his way up on a newspaper until he was a syndicated column of his own. He doesn't need a fortune. What he genuinely welcomes is the challenge of hard work.

Nevertheless he eyed the radiant and revealing faces with a kind of foreboding and said nothing to indicate that their secret was no secret at all. He would wait until they were ready to confide in him, but he hoped their attitude toward each other would not be as apparent to others as it was to himself.

Jane told them about Mrs. Toyman's visit and her urgent request that Jane stay with her until the case was cleared up. "She's so awfully kind and so lonely. Now the Christmas list is ready, she doesn't have much of anything to do and she never really had many friends. Her whole life has centered on the business and making a home for her husband. And Chris and I both suspected that he discouraged any kind of social life because of the expense involved. Everything had to go back into the business."

"You aren't going to accept her invitation?" Forsyth said in alarm.

"Oh, no. I told her the police wouldn't let me and why. She was horrified about the abduction and said she wished she could keep me safe. But I explained I had Mrs. Talent, who is a whole army in herself," and Jane smiled across the table at the policewoman.

"You," Forsyth said firmly, "are going to stay right here," saw the compression of Jane's lips and the policewoman's shake of the head. "Sorry, dear, I can't seem to remember that you have grown up."

"Just not broken to the saddle," Mike said. "It takes a lot of skill and patience to train these young colts to obedience."

"Why, you—!"

Mike laughed, his eyes exultant when he looked at her, but his voice had its usual mocking tone of one who took nothing seriously. Then he told Forsyth about his interviews with Tilson and Beverly.

"Beverly! It's only fair to confess I went down for the

count! What charm. What beauty. What technique. Now there's a woman for you."

Jane picked up a roll and menaced him with it.

"Children, children," Forsyth said plaintively, but he added seriously, "Mike, for God's sake, keep out of this. Did you hear about Jane's second telephone call? Don't go on."

Something in his tone made the policewoman give him a sharp look of speculation.

"Just the same," Mike said, and he was serious too, "that woman knows something. She hasn't got an alibi for sour apples and she's up to something. I'd give an arm and a leg to know what it is."

II

Not far away, Mrs. Harrison Fitch was facing a tall girl dressed in black but without the dramatic widow's veil.

"Just what are you trying to tell me, Miss—uh—"

"Beverly Barker. For five months I was Mrs. Chester Loring." There was insolence in the girl's stance, in her expression, in her voice. "I don't know what name you knew him under."

Mrs. Fitch reached for a bell cord beside her chair and Beverly was beside her in one long stride, gripping her arm. "Oh, no, you don't. You don't have me thrown out. I'll leave when I am ready and I won't leave until I get what I came for. And don't yell. You'll bring this house right down around your ears and raise more dust than you've ever seen before. The great Mrs. Harrison Fitch, social leader, patron of charities, sponsor of medical research, homes in Cannes, Switzerland, England. An apartment in Paris and one in Rome."

"If you think for one moment, young woman—"

Beverly brushed the words aside. "Sister, let's talk business. I don't forget faces. For several years I've modeled dresses for you and seen you at our opening shows. You're one of Biltmore's best customers, always invited to our pre-season showings. I know your measurements and I know your taste, good but conservative.

"So all of a sudden you pop off the society page and show up for Chester's funeral, hiding behind dark glasses. They threw me off for a moment but, hell, I remembered the dress and the way you walk. So I begin to wonder what brings you to the funeral service for a guy like Chester, who wasn't in your social class. And I can think of only one reason. He was one of your—shall I say private charities? Who gave Chester a fistful of twenties? His boss didn't pay him in cash. Little Jane didn't have control of her money. I wouldn't have supported him even if I could. That's no way to get a man and hold him, not the way I want to hold one. So I got to thinking. Here's one dame who is well heeled and here we have a lady who does a vanishing act from a motel, and I put two and two together."

Mrs. Fitch, gripping the arms of her chair, managed to get to her feet. Even at this moment she had a great deal of dignity.

Beverly was not impressed by the stricken face. "Sit down, sister. I'm here to talk money. I'm likely to lose my job over this business, what with having no alibi and, like a fool, involving my boss. So I need money to tide me over, plenty of it, enough to keep me until I can get set somewhere else. I may have to go to Chicago or California or Dallas, or the Lord knows where."

Mrs. Fitch's lips opened without sound. Then she cleared her throat and said distinctly, "Not a penny."

Beverly moved in a leisurely way toward the door, pausing to say, "There's no hurry. Think it over until, say, Friday morning. That will give you tomorrow to get the cash in hand. I'll need about fifteen thousand."

"This is preposterous. It's blackmail."

"So?"

"Why should I?"

"Because I can guess what was with you and Chester. Sex and cash."

"Guess?" Mrs. Fitch managed a laugh. "To make a story like that stick would require evidence, wouldn't it, and you don't have any."

Beverly's brows arched. "I'll call you on Friday. Promptly at noon. I'll tell you then where and how to leave the money. I won't pick it up here; I'm not walking into any trap. In fact, a trap is the last thing you'll want too, sister. Because I can blow your fine reputation sky-high and cover you with so much mud you'll never get clean again." Beverly nodded and went out of the room with her long graceful stride.

Mrs. Harrison Fitch sat staring straight ahead of her while the long summer twilight faded and lights began to appear in the buildings around her. The shock occasioned by Beverly had faded; she was deep in thought, considering, rejecting, looking for a way out of the cobweb in which she was entangled. It came down, after all, to only one possibility. It was a risk, of course, but at this point everything was a risk. At length she searched her telephone directory and made a call, a fairly brief call. Again she sat staring out at the lights that were beginning to transform New York, make it magical, unaware of her own surroundings, of the darkened room in which she sat.

At last she went to her bedroom on the floor above, a lovely room whose four-poster bed had a satin cover that matched the draperies. She switched on a light and began searching through bureau drawers. At length she found a small pearl-handled revolver. Automatically she adjusted a trim hat, checked her discreet makeup, picked up her gloves and the handbag into which she dropped the revolver. Then she switched off the light, went briskly down the stairs, and out into the street.

III

When dinner was over, Forsyth settled down in his bookroom and made no comment when Mike suggested casually that Jane join him in the drawing room for a game of gin rummy. The policewoman sat in the television room. It was certainly true that everything seemed more dramatic in color. She'd talk to Jake about it.

Forsyth started to write a letter and then put down his pen. There were other, more pressing things on his mind than inquiring about the unusual chess set he'd seen in a catalog. He drummed his fingers on the desk. He hated what he had to do, but Jane came first, Jane and Mike. He had liked Hank Fitch, liked him a lot. Theirs had been an unusually close friendship with a number of shared interests and a similar point of view on most important issues. Since Jane's marriage and Hank's death he had come to know Mrs. Fitch better. Over conservative for his taste, but a woman of charm and breeding, with an interesting mind.

Well, it had to be done. He rang the precinct in whose jurisdiction the Lawrence murder was being handled and, after identifying himself, said he'd like to speak to someone in authority on the case as he had some information that might be relevant. Of course, it might be merely a red herring, but he didn't feel it was up to him to decide.

The man he reached was new to him but not new to the case. In fact, he had the folder in front of him as he talked.

"What can we do for you, Mr. Forsyth?"

"I think it is probably—possibly—a case of what I can do

for you. One of your men suggested that I might be able to find out where Mrs. Harrison Fitch banks and whether or not she had made any large withdrawals."

"Mrs. Harrison Fitch!" The man's excitement surprised Forsyth.

"Yes. She banks at the Glenville and a friend of mine there, who would prefer not to be identified—he's right at the top—told me that some two years ago Mrs. Fitch withdrew twenty thousand dollars in twenty-dollar bills. She explained that the money was intended for an indigent relative who had to have an expensive operation and a long period for recuperation and was too proud to accept help. This was the only way she could manage it without his knowing of her assistance. At the time the bank teller suspected blackmail, but he had no recourse but to give her the money. She filled a briefcase with it."

"I see. Yes, I see. That figures."

"According to my banker friend, there have been no big withdrawals since then. So apparently she is clear of any complicity in the Lawrence case. She certainly didn't supply the money he is said to have been flourishing around, for which, thank God! Hank Fitch was one of my most valued friends and I hate like hell doing this to his widow. I suppose I should have called her first and warned her of what I was going to do."

"Well, I don't think it would make any difference. You couldn't have reached her, Mr. Forsyth."

"What do you mean by that?"

"Mrs. Fitch is in a hospital emergency ward where she was taken after being found unconscious just inside the entrance to Central Park, lying under some bushes. She'd been struck over the temple; same M.O. as in the Lawrence death. It could be the same weapon. We're not sure yet, of course, but there's a striking similarity."

"Well, I'll be damned. What hospital? The least I can do is send some flowers."

"She won't know the difference for a couple of days, if she ever does. There's no hurry about it. And I might as well tell you this, as the newsmen have got hold of it already. She had a revolver in her hand from which one shot had been fired. That's how the police found her so soon. Heard the shot. But thank you for calling, Mr. Forsyth."

"My God! No indication that she hit anyone?"

"Well, we haven't found a bullet. If that's all—"

"Oh, there's one more thing while I am at it. I have instructed my bank to give you any information you may require about my own financial situation. You are bound to think of it, of course. As a matter of fact, if you could read my mind, where that bastard Lawrence is concerned, you'd be sure I was guilty."

The policeman laughed. "Usually our murderers aren't so forthcoming. I'm not letting any cat out of the bag, Mr. Forsyth, but your niece has had a couple of bad shocks. I'm not implying anything, understand?"

"Well?"

"You've got Hilda Talent there. Tell her not to let a woman named Beverly Barker near Miss Forsyth."

"Are you implying—"

"I'm not implying anything. All we know is that Beverly Barker is the last person known to have seen Mrs. Fitch before she walked out of her house three hours ago. No word to her servants about dinner. Nothing. Just walked out."

IV

It was Forsyth who carried the information to Jane and Mike, who were talking earnestly, with cards spread out before them, which they were making no pretense of playing.

They looked up from their enchanted absorption in each other when Forsyth came in, calling as he passed the television room, "You'd better hear this, Mrs. Talent."

When she had joined them, he waved her to a chair and stood leaning against the mantel.

"I just talked to the police. I told them I'd looked up Mrs. Harrison Fitch's banker and found that she withdrew twenty thousand dollars in twenties two years ago on a trumped-up excuse. They expected at the time that it was extortion, but they had no right to prevent her spending her money as she chose."

"I thought it had to be that way," Jane said. "She was the only one with the money and the reason for paying out blackmail. I wish I hadn't told her I knew."

"I wish you hadn't either, honey, but it's too late."

"At least I can tell her I am sorry."

"Not if she's a murderer and a kidnaper," Mike put in harshly.

"She seems to be the only one who can be eliminated from suspicion," Forsyth said heavily. "She was found unconscious just inside Central Park tonight, with a blow on her temple like that on Lawrence's head. She is unconscious and they don't know whether she'll ever wake up again."

Only Mrs. Talent did not join in the exclamations of horror. She was alert, watching Forsyth's every expression. "You thought I should be in on this. Why, Mr. Forsyth?"

"Because the police want you to make sure that in no circumstance is Beverly Barker to get near my niece. She was the last person to see Mrs. Fitch before the latter walked out of her house three hours ago. All the police know, and the thing that led them to her so quickly, is that she fired one bullet at someone and the bullet hasn't been found. Looks as though it hit a target."

"So it's Beverly," Jane began bewilderedly. "But why? It

doesn't make sense. Why would she want to kill me after Chris is gone? Why?"

"They didn't say she was the killer, did they?" Hilda Talent said. "No, I thought not. But extortion is something else." She was silent for some time. Then she turned to Jane. "Did you go through—your husband's—things after his death?"

"Yes. Well, no. Mike did it for me."

"What did you do with them?"

"Left them, along with Jane's clothes, the furniture, and the food, for the superintendent. He has a big family to support."

"Find any letters?"

Mike shook his head. "There wasn't a single paper, not an address book, not a letter, not even a business memorandum. I thought it was odd at the time. He seemed to be covering his tracks."

"Did he ever give you any papers to keep for him?" Mrs. Talent asked Jane.

Jane shook her head. "And he never got any mail. I thought it must go to his business address."

Again the policewoman was silent, brooding, and no one interrupted her meditations. She did no wool-gathering, as they had learned. "That's got to be it,' she said at last. "I can't see Mrs. Fitch killing anyone. But I can see her paying out her life's blood to prevent scandal. Dollars to doughnuts she wrote letters. Those 'Precious Sweetie' things that crop up in divorce cases. That would account for her attempt to get rid of you. She thought you had them. Then she learned about the other wife: She's the one who searched Beverly's studio. Then Beverly showed her hand, threatened her with exposure. She must have fired that shot before she was struck. I'd like to know what Beverly looks like now. You can't conceal bullet wounds with cosmetics."

V

It was late when Mike pulled Jane to her feet. "I don't want to let you go, but you're tired and you need rest. See you in the morning." He started to push her toward the stairs, took her in his arms instead, rocking her, kissing her eyes, her cheeks, her throat, her lips.

When he released her, breathless and half laughing, she said in wonder, "How can anything happen like this so fast? Like lightning."

"Lightning, nothing. I've been in love with you since you were ten years old with braces on your teeth and freckles on your nose. Here and here." He kissed the spots. "But you thought I was a big brother."

"A big brute most of the time. No!" as he reached for her again. "Mrs. Talent will be down here and run you in, if you aren't careful."

"Good night, darling. Remember you're safe. Nothing can hurt you now."

As he started back to mix a nightcap, his words were justified as Johnson came through to check the lock on the front door and all the windows, one hand resting suggestively on his pocket.

Mike laughed. "Good God, do you go around the house with that gun?"

"Yes, sir. Anyone who gets past me—"

"There's a tall blonde named Beverly Barker who was also married to Lawrence. She's a troublemaker. Don't let her in, no matter what excuse she offers. She is not to get near Miss Forsyth."

"She won't get a foot inside the door," Johnson promised.

19

ABOUT THE only thing to develop the following morning was the information that Mrs. Harrison Fitch would not be able to testify about her assailant for a long, long time. She lay white and still on her hospital bed, only the vital functions, still faintly registering, indicating that she lived.

A protesting doctor had finally been persuaded to let a member of the police look at her and he had been aware, at a glance, that there was no way of gleaning from her what she knew.

"When will she be able to talk?" he asked at length.

The doctor shrugged. "Perhaps never. She has about a forty per cent chance of living, about a ten per cent chance of remembering."

"But there is some chance," the policeman persisted.

"As long as she is alive."

"We've got to keep her alive, doctor. We'll be putting one of our men on guard outside her door, three eight-hour shifts a day, until we know one way or another."

"That is impossible. It would demoralize hospital routine. And the woman is safe enough here. We'll advise you the moment there is any indication of returning consciousness."

"There's been one murder, one attempted murder, one abduction that was intended to end in murder. We can't take a chance. If you don't want a uniformed man at her door, we'll send along a woman operative and you can put her in a nurse's uniform. But we want this door guarded at all times. Please leave clear instructions that anyone entering the room must provide some identification to show to our operative. Okay?"

"Is it that serious?"

The policeman looked down at the motionless body on the bed, whose only sign of life was the faint rising and falling of her chest. "What do you think?"

II

The story hit the morning papers, radio and television. There was no suggestion that the injury to Mrs. Harrison Fitch had any bearing on the murder of Charles Lawrence. Her social and financial position was such that her accident was front-page material and brought forth the usual spate of talk about the need of increased safety in the city parks. There was no comment about the revolver she had carried and which was found in her hand and from which a bullet had been fired.

That was revealed in the afternoon papers. At the same time there was a story about the similarity between the wounds on Lawrence and Mrs. Fitch, apparently made by the same weapon. There was no indication, though boundless speculation, about what it could be.

And there it rested.

Meanwhile the inexorable routine went on. Men armed with warrants searched every inch of Mrs. Fitch's house, to the consternation of her staff, already stunned by the knowledge that she lay near death as the result of a brutal attack in Central Park, where she had apparently shot her assailant.

"But," her tearful maid reiterated over and over, "she would never have gone into the park alone after dark. Never in the world."

"Then how did she get there?" the detective questioning her asked wearily.

On her dressing table, while the maid watched sharply to make sure nothing was taken, the detective picked up a framed picture of a Swiss chalet. He looked at it curiously. Pretty enough but not what you'd expect on a dressing table where women were more likely to keep family portraits.

"That's Madam's place in Switzerland," the maid explained. "She spends about a month there every year. Three years ago she took me along because I'd been run-down from flu. It was wonderful. Those mountains! And all the flowers. Just everywhere."

He nodded, turned the picture over, saw a narrow edge of cardboard sticking up, and pulled it out. It was a picture of a young man with long blond hair, wearing only a singlet and shorts, and laughing into the camera.

The maid, looking over his shoulder, gasped.

"Ever see this before?"

"I never knew it was there! But I've seen him. He used to come here, oh, several years ago it was, and he'd call for her and they'd go out. I asked once if he was a nephew of hers and she looked sort of funny and said he was the son of an old friend in town just for a few months and she had been asked to be nice to him. And then after a while I guess he went away, though I have a feeling I saw him somewhere not long ago. Someone like him anyhow. But not here. You'd never forget him. Just a dream."

Probably the picture of him taken after his death, the detective thought.

"Does Mrs. Fitch carry much money with her as a rule?"

"Usually less than fifty dollars, but she had a lot of charge accounts, of course; most of the big stores and the best restaurants."

"Jewelry?"

"Lots of it and just beautiful, but she keeps it in her bank unless she is planning to dress formal. Never wears anything daytime except her wedding and engagement rings and a plain sort of watch, and maybe her pearls."

"She had all that and about thirty-six dollars in her handbag. And a pearl-handled revolver in her hand. Did you ever see a revolver in this house?"

"Mrs. Fitch had a revolver? Mrs. Fitch!"

The detective checked a flow of incredulity and tried to pin her down. At last, after assuring him that Mr. Fitch had never been one for guns, he trusted to burglar alarms in the city and in the country he kept two big dogs. But a pearl-handled revolver—there was something now she came to think of it—oh, yes, a friend of theirs was held up when he was garaging his car one night in East Hampton and he told Mr. Fitch it wouldn't have happened if he had kept a gun in his car pocket. So Mr. Fitch got this revolver for his wife and made her learn how to use it and though she did it to relieve his mind—she is such a kind, thoughtful lady—she put it away after his death. She hated guns and violence in any form.

The detective phoned in his findings at the Fitch house which, he admitted, amounted to damn little. He was informed that reporters had descended on the hospital where Mrs. Fitch lay unconscious. The woman operative in a trim white nurse's uniform sat outside her room and inspected the identification of everyone coming in. Some of the newsmen had tried all sorts of tricks, one getting hold of an intern's coat, but the policewoman had recognized him. The chief drawback was that Ida Franklin was a smart policewoman but she was so darned attractive that the hospital complained the interns were hanging around her instead of going on their rounds.

"Hey," the detective said, "I've staked out Ida for myself.

Just waiting to pass the next examination to get things set up with her."

"You'd better hurry, man." The voice at the end of the telephone laughed. "You've got competition around here as well as at the hospital. Oh—what's that?—yeah, you're to get onto Beverly Barker. We're sending a policewoman to meet you on the street outside her building. She'll search the girl. You know what you're looking for."

"Why not do it the other way?" the detective asked. "Women are better at searching houses."

"On your way. You'll be meeting Opal Young."

The detective groaned. Opal was a good shot and a good cop but she wasn't in the same league with Ida. However, Beverly wouldn't be able to put anything over on her.

III

Opal Young was almost as tall as Detective Smith and considerably broader through the middle, though there was no fat on her; she was all muscle. She was in uniform as she had been told that would be the most effective approach with a girl like Beverly Barker.

She nodded in a businesslike way as Smith drove up. "We've got to climb four flights," she told him and began trudging up the uncarpeted stairs. At the door of the studio she knocked briskly.

This morning Beverly Barker wore thin white slacks and a pale yellow blouse. There were sandals on her feet. For once she was not attempting to be seductive. Her pallor increased as she looked from face to face.

"More cops. Okay. Let's get it over with."

The policewoman summed her up in one shrewd look and took a swift overall summary of the room. There were indications that a hurried attempt had been made to straighten it. The studio couch had been made up, the dishes were stacked in the sink, clothes were out of sight. Spread out on the card table was the tabloid with its headline:

MRS. FITCH STILL UNCONSCIOUS
UNDER GUARD IN HOSPITAL

The policewoman with the unlikely name of Opal ducked her head at Smith. "There's only the one room. You can wait outside until I call you."

He nodded and went out without a word.

Beverly was alarmed. "Hey, what is this all about?"

Opal nodded toward the newspaper. "I guess you have as good an idea as I have. All right, sister, I want you to strip. Everything."

Beverly backed away. "Why? Do you have a warrant for this?"

"I sure have." Opal produced it. "This is no pleasure to me. It's just a job."

"But what—God, you can see I haven't anything under my pants and shirt."

"Take them off and let's not waste time. And don't tell me you haven't taken off your clothes in front of an audience before now."

"Not women," Beverly said, outraged, and the policewoman grinned.

"Don't let that worry you. Okay, do you take them off or do I?"

Beverly sullenly removed her shirt and her slacks. The policewoman looked at her, told her to turn around, no, more slowly. Hold it. At length she nodded. "Okay, you can put them on again."

"And what was that all about? And what did you think I could have concealed on my bare hide?"

"A bullet hole," Opal informed her.

"A bul—" For a moment Beverly was too astonished to speak. Then she crumpled and sat down on the couch, her head in her hands. "Oh, God! If that isn't just like my luck! First I lose Chester and then I lose my job, and now—Look!" She did not even notice that Smith had returned, after a cautious glance in her direction.

"Go to it," the policewoman instructed him, and he began a meticulous search of the kitchenette.

"You know what it's about, don't you?" Opal said.

"I don't know what you are looking for. That's God's truth. Someone was ahead of you. If it wasn't the police, who was it? What am I supposed to be hiding, for God's sake? The crown jewels?"

"You're the last person known to have seen Mrs. Harrison Fitch alive," Opal told her.

"Alive! God, you don't mean she is dead?"

"She's still alive. No one knows yet whether she'll recover or, even if she does, whether she will remember anything."

Smith was prodding in cans of sugar, coffee, and flour and for a moment Beverly's attention was distracted. "Don't spill anything. It's hell to get it out of that cracked old linoleum." She turned to the policewoman. "I read the paper and I heard last night's news. I figured then that the police would come after me, sooner or later. But I can tell you this—I swear it's true—Mrs. Fitch never took a shot at me last night. Whoever she went to the park to meet, it wasn't me. I wanted her alive. God, how I wanted her alive!"

"Extortion?"

"Prove it," Beverly said listlessly. "She can't talk."

"It's about the only defense you have against a murder charge."

"But she's not dead."

"Lawrence is. And you haven't an alibi for his death or Jane Forsyth's abduction or the attack on Mrs. Fitch last

182

night. Do you want to talk? Read her her rights, Smith."

He did so and Beverly nodded. "Yeah, I know. I have a right to remain silent or to call a lawyer, but that won't keep me out of jail, will it?"

"So cut your losses," the policewoman advised her, as Smith moved on to the small bathroom to continue his search.

"What in hell are you looking for?" Beverly demanded.

"The weapon that killed Lawrence and nearly killed Mrs. Fitch."

"You won't find it here. Chester was a doll. A perfect doll." Tears swam in her eyes. "I loved the guy. I don't say he was the first in my life, but he was the only one who counted. I was willing to live like this if that was what he wanted. He was—" She wiped her eyes and blew her nose on a tissue which she crumpled and tossed inaccurately at a wastebasket. "As for the Forsyth girl, she came here and practically threatened me and suggested maybe she could find where I really was when Chester died. And that's the last I ever saw of her except at the funeral service. And she didn't even send flowers! I guess that shows you."

"And Mrs. Fitch?"

At Smith's suggestion the two women moved to the card table while he searched the couch, prodding under the cushions, opening it out, searching the bedding. Then he rolled it away from the wall, looking at the curled dust on the floor. Beverly was so engaged in watching his activities that she momentarily forgot Opal, who continued to study her with intent, disillusioned eyes.

"Now to get back to Mrs. Fitch."

"Okay. Well, they kept hammering at me."

"Who did?"

"First the cops wanting to know where I was when Chester was killed."

"And you said you were doing legitimate work with your agent who had a jealous wife."

Beverly made no reply.

"Well?"

"And then Baby Jane appears. She hasn't got an alibi herself so she's out to find out who else is without one. She thinks she can do it and she has the nerve to tell me the police don't believe mine." She waited for Opal's comment but there was none. "So then Baby Jane's cousin arrives on the scene—"

"And he blows your alibi sky-high."

"And the Biltmore Mart telephones to say politely that my employment has been terminated, and a confirming letter will be sent, along with two weeks' extra pay in lieu of vacation money and no references. And I was going to be sent to Paris!" This was a wail, the realest emotion she had displayed yet.

"So you decide to retrieve your fortune through Mrs. Fitch." The policewoman believed in cutting red tape and getting on with it. "Why?"

Beverly hesitated for a moment but she was not, the policewoman believed, trying to think up a likely story. She was simply trying to marshal her facts.

"Well, I got to thinking about the money. All that money Chester was said to be carrying around with him. So where did it come from? Not from Baby Jane, who couldn't put her hands on her own money or he'd have got it all right." There was no criticism in Beverly's voice, a simple acceptance of the facts of life. "Not from me. I didn't need to pay any man! I always had my pick. But then I remembered the people who had come to the service for Chester. I have a good memory for faces and, in spite of her dark glasses and the dim light, I recognized Mrs. Fitch by her walk, and anyhow I'd modeled that dress for her.

"Well, I ask you! Mrs. Harrison Fitch! Fifty if she's a day and like the Cabots and the Lodges, and she shows up at Chester's funeral wearing dark glasses. So it adds up to just one thing. Chester played up to her, pulled out the charm, and she was at the age to fall for it. And she's loaded. So, without a job or a husband or anything—and," again that heartbroken wail, "practically on my way to Paris, I figured I had something coming to me."

She broke off as Detective Smith sat down on the couch and pulled out his notebook. "And now will you kindly tell me what the hell you were looking for?"

"Miss Barker," Opal said, "did your—did Lawrence ever give you any documents, letters, anything like that to keep for him?"

Beverly blinked, shook her head. "I don't think he ever got a letter all the time we were married. I just assumed they went to wherever he worked."

"And you didn't know where it was?"

"To tell you the truth, I didn't give a damn. So, like the song says, he was my man and he done me wrong, but I'd do it all over again."

"Let's go back," Opal said. "You figured you had something coming to you."

"You know already I went to see Mrs. Fitch. You can read the score as well as me. I told her I knew about her and Chester. I knew he must have got that money from her. I knew she must have been the woman in the motel. I asked for a few thousand and said I'd call her on Friday, giving her today to collect the money. So she gets herself nearly killed."

"And now," the policewoman said briskly, "let's have a few nice clean alibis from you. Something that will stand up in court. Because you're in trouble, sister. Real bad trouble."

"I know it. I knew when I read about Mrs. Fitch's accident that her servants would remember me going there and insisting on seeing her. But I never told her to meet me in the park."

"Where were you when Lawrence was killed, when Jane Forsyth was abducted, when Mrs. Fitch was attacked last night?"

Beverly had been gripping her hands together. Now they dropped lax at her sides. She took a long breath and her voice was dull. "Okay, I had an abortion the night Chester was killed. I didn't expect him home until sometime this week. Afterwards I came home and crawled into bed. That's where I was most of the time until I went to the funeral. I knew Chester wouldn't like—encumbrances, responsibilities. And a baby would maybe ruin my figure and keep me from modeling for a long time. And someone would have to look after the brat. Well, I mean I'm just not cut out to be a mother. And last evening I went back for a checkup. I can give you the doctor's name." She wrote out a name and address and handed it to the policewoman. "And now, could you, for God's sake, leave me alone. I've just about had it."

"Yes, I guess you have. All right, kid. Take it easy. It looks like you're in the clear on everything but attempted extortion and you are safe on that until—or unless—Mrs. Fitch recovers."

The policewoman nodded to Smith and the two went down the stairs to the street, where Smith looked at the sky. "Clouding up. I hope it rains. It might drop the temperature some."

"At least it might clear the air," Opal said and climbed in the police car.

20

THERE WAS a lot to be said for youth, Hilda Talent acknowledged to herself, watching Jane's rapid comeback from a state of near collapse to a happiness that made her eyes bright, her skin glow, and restored the spring to her step. Not, Hilda admitted, that she would care to relive her youth. It had been tough going, but there was no doubt that the younger you were, the quicker you could snap back.

Just the same, until the case was settled—and the accident to Mrs. Fitch had indicated that somewhere the murderer was still at large—Jane had better learn a little discretion.

The door to Jane's sitting room was no longer locked and she had the run of the house though she did not attempt to leave it.

When Mike had set off on an undisclosed errand, Hilda looked at the smiling girl, who was lost in delighted dreams. "Watch it," she said. "Be careful about the way you look at that guy or, like the song says, people will think you are in love." Then she added seriously, "I don't want to disturb love's young dream but neither of you is out of the woods, kid. So don't give the police any more to think about."

She had effectively banished Jane's state of euphoria. "What do you think, Mrs. Talent?"

"You're clean and so is your cousin. At least I'm pretty sure of him by now."

"But not entirely sure?"

"Well, of all the people involved he's the one who had the strongest motive. He was in love with you and he wanted to get rid of Lawrence. Anyone can see that."

"You don't really suspect him," Jane said after thinking it over. "He'd never have had a part in that abduction scheme. He wouldn't have hurt Mrs. Fitch."

"No, I don't really suspect him but I wouldn't stake my life on it. The police like evidence. Up to now there is only one person in this whole affair who has alibis to cover everything."

"Who's that?"

"Beverly Barker. I've just been talking to the precinct. She was having an abortion while Lawrence was getting himself killed."

"Oh, the poor thing! The poor thing! How awful for her."

"According to the report I got, she thought Lawrence wouldn't welcome encumbrances or responsibilities and she doesn't seem to be a case of frustrated motherhood."

"So she couldn't have killed Chris or abducted me or tried to kill Mrs. Fitch."

"Has it occurred to you that there might be several people involved? That the murder and the abduction and the attack on Mrs. Fitch might not all be the work of the same person?"

"But why?"

"I don't know why. Your uncle hasn't an alibi that stands up for your husband's murder and he had as strong a motive as your cousin. He wanted you free."

"He wouldn't," Jane said firmly.

"And then there is Mr. Toyman, whose alibi for the night of the murder is based only on the testimony of his wife, which doesn't count for much."

"Oh, for heaven's sake," Jane said in exasperation. "Why on earth would Mr. Toyman want to kill Chris? He was his best salesman. He was going to turn the business over to him when he retires."

"Who said so until after Lawrence was killed?"

"Chris told me so."

"Did he?" Hilda said in a curious tone.

"And when Mike and I went there after Chris was dead Mr. Toyman told me he had planned to turn the business over to Chris."

"That was after Lawrence was dead."

"And Mrs. Toyman herself said her husband was home the night Chris died; he had an abscessed tooth. She wouldn't stand for any shenanigans any more than her husband would. Why, they had been married for twenty-five years, and anyhow, you could have told for yourself what she was like when she came here."

"Twenty-five years of Jittery Joe, as Forman calls him, would be enough for any woman. Must have married him when she was about twenty. He's—what? Seventy? No kids. Nothing but the business and the designs she makes for children's toys. I wonder if she married him just because he had a toyshop?"

"But don't you remember? The ideas were hers."

Hilda Talent held up her hand to silence Jane's chatter. "Let me think." After a few minutes during which Jane was respectfully silent, the policewoman said, "I heard what Mrs. Toyman said when she was here. Her husband had a marvelous offer and intended to sell out. They would move to El Paso where living was cheap and she'd have nothing to do but sit around and knit. But suppose he'd had that offer some time ago. Suppose," and the policewoman put up a big square hand to silence Jane, "Mrs. Toyman didn't want to be left out of a business that was her own creation. Suppose she figured that she and Lawrence could carry on together."

"And then she killed him?"

"I didn't say that."

"Who else? Oh, you mean Mr. Toyman? But that's crazy."

"Lawrence's killer wasn't crazy. He was careful and he took his time. He left no evidence. If he was also your abductor, he made only one slip when he put you in the car of an abandoned house and told you that it was. So there's a direct link from Giddings to Lawrence to Toyman."

"But why? Why?"

"Because Mrs. Toyman didn't want to sell out. She wanted to go into business with Lawrence. Or shall I put it another way? She wanted Lawrence."

"Oh!" Jane sounded as though the breath had been knocked out of her. "Mrs. Toyman?" she said wonderingly. "But she's been like a mother to us."

"Were those her words or Toyman's?"

Jane did not answer, trying to absorb a new and unpalatable idea.

Hilda nodded. "A cruel thing to do, if it was Toyman needling his wife."

"But—"

"Look, kid, take off those rose-colored glasses. You know the score about Lawrence by now. You know about Mrs. Fitch, who paid for him. If there was one, there could be others. A woman of forty-five married to a man of seventy, a woman who—and I heard her myself—had never known any romance, who could lay her hands on a nice piece of money—"

Jane sat down limply. "You think Mrs. Toyman could have been the woman registered as Mrs. Carl Lamb at the motel? That she was the one who gave Chris all that money?"

"It's a possibility, isn't it?"

"Then who took the money? Who killed him? Who abducted me? Who—?"

"Whoa. I've got a theory, dearie. Just a theory. Let's

suppose Toyman gets an offer to sell out. He is old and ready to quit and live easily on the profits. But she is young middle-age and still teeming with ideas and she wants to carry on —with the right partner. And there is Lawrence ready to provide the partnership and the romance or whatever—for a price. So she makes a big withdrawal in cash from her bank. And if I know anything about Toyman, he knows where every penny goes. So he follows her to the motel. He gets in that room by some trick, checking on fire, whatever, kills Lawrence, removes his wallet and all identification and gets out, taking his wife with him. And she doesn't dare open her trap. How's that?"

"Why doesn't she if she knows he is the murderer?"

"Because there is only one way Lawrence and Mrs. Toyman could go into partnership. By eliminating Toyman. He can figure that out for himself. So he gets his lick in first."

"Then why did she want me to go to New Jersey to keep me safe?"

"To keep herself safe by having a witness on hand. It's not a bad theory, is it?" The policewoman smiled. "There's one way we can find out how much truth there is in it."

"What's that?" Jane was cautious.

"Your uncle pulled some strings and found out about Mrs. Fitch's bank account. Maybe he could do the same thing for the Toymans. And if you want to bet a fiver, I'll lay mine on Mrs. Toyman having a separate account. Any takers?"

"Well, maybe she has," Jane said cautiously. "Chris said Mr. Toyman gave her a percentage on everything she designed and she was putting it away in the old teapot. That was just the way he put it. Said she liked nice things and Toyman wanted them to put everything back into the business. She's the one, Chris said, who bought the Bentley. He was furious about it and said they could have had a car for a quarter of the cost and a quarter of the expense of upkeep."

"We've got ourselves a working theory. Let's take it up with Mr. Forsyth."

"He's gone out to see that criminal lawyer again. He wants me to talk to him tonight."

"He's sure way ahead of time in calling out the heavy artillery," Hilda commented, her voice colorless. "They were speculating about it at the precinct."

"If you think for one minute," Jane flared, "that Uncle Jim has anything to hide—"

"Everyone has something to hide," Hilda replied, unimpressed.

II

Forsyth and Mike returned to the house at the same time. As they sat at lunch, Hilda noticed that Forsyth was quiet and Mike was in high spirits. He had had a long talk with Ivan the Terrible, who had checked with the police and was going to give the story of Jane's abduction a big play.

"After all," Mike said, "the abductor knows all about it. Who are we concealing it from?"

"From whom," Jane corrected him.

He ignored her. "I ought to get a raise out of this."

"Anyone would think you were a combination of Cronkite and Chancellor," Jane commented.

"Another crack like that and you may not be asked to share my rosy future. On second thought, I'm not sure you're the right wife for a coming man."

"Cummins wants to see you when he comes here tonight," Forsyth said abruptly. "He doesn't like the way you are trying to run this case."

"I can take care of myself."

"And Jane?"

Mike was silent. He was also deflated.

It wasn't like Uncle Jim, Jane thought, to snub Mike that

way. Hurriedly she began to discuss Mrs. Talent's theory about the murder, with Chris taking Mrs. Toyman to the motel, the latter providing funds, and Toyman breaking in to kill Chris, retrieve the money, get his wife out of there, and forestall any attempt on the part of the two of them to get rid of him.

"It's a horrible idea," she admitted, "but Mrs. Talent thought maybe you'd have a way of checking, finding out whether Mrs. Toyman really did withdraw a lot of money in hundred-dollar bills."

"Toyman. That old fussbudget!" Mike exclaimed. "I could think of a dozen better theories than that."

Forsyth made an impatient gesture. "I could probably learn something about the Toyman banking situation."

Johnson came in. "There are two men from the police at the door. I saw their identifications. They have warrants to search the house."

There was a moment of stunned silence and then Forsyth put down his napkin and got to his feet. "Of course. Give them any assistance you can, Johnson." He turned to Mrs. Talent. "What do they want?"

"I don't know, sir. They haven't said anything to me. So far as I can make out, there are two sets of people searching; someone had searched Beverly Barker's studio before the police got around to it."

"Two sets of people!" Mike exclaimed. "Why?"

"I'd guess that someone wants any letters that Lawrence may have cached somewhere and the police are looking for the murder weapon."

Mike laughed. "That's easy. The killer dropped it in the East River. Why hold onto it?"

"It's an interesting point, isn't it, especially as we know it's been used twice and is probably still—available."

Mike blinked, wet his lips, and for once he was silent. His

exuberance was gone, his usual healthy appetite failed him, and he pushed the food around on his plate without eating.

After lunch they sat in the bookroom, not trying to talk, frankly listening to the sounds of men moving quietly through the upstairs rooms. One of them came down and signaled to Mrs. Talent, who followed them out for a low-toned colloquy. When she returned, three pairs of eyes searched her face.

For a moment she was silent and then she said, "You might as well know. They wanted to know whether I had searched Miss Forsyth's suite and I said I had, every single inch."

"I didn't know that," Jane said.

"I did most of it while you were sleeping or when you were out of your rooms." She grinned. "You're clean."

Forsyth reached for the telephone. "I'm getting Cummins here this minute."

"If you think it advisable, Mr. Forsyth," the policewoman said quietly. "The cops are just doing their job, you know."

He looked at her and drew back his hand. A moment later he said restlessly, "I don't hear them. Where are they now?"

"Looking through your bedroom, Mr. Forsyth."

"Oh." He looked around him aimlessly. "What was I— I was going to put out some feelers on the Toyman banking arrangements." This time he reached for the telephone with more confidence.

Jane and Mike, followed by Mrs. Talent, went into the drawing room. This afternoon the policewoman was not to be beguiled from her duty by the most enthralling of soap operas. Like the other two she listened to the men walking around upstairs. One of them came down and began to look through the dining room. The other had gone into Mike's room. The dining room finished, the first man tackled the television room, a brief process, and then went into the butler's pantry, where he talked to Mrs. Johnson in a cheerful voice, assuring her he wasn't going to mess things up, working quickly and efficiently.

From upstairs there came a loud exclamation and then a clatter of feet on the stairs. The man from the pantry went to join his colleague, followed by Mrs. Talent.

Mike and Jane got up, straining to see the object which the detective was holding by a small pair of tongs.

"Could be," the other man said. "Could be. But what the hell is it?"

"You've got me."

"Where did you find it?"

"A pocket in one of Heald's suits." The two policemen and Mrs. Talent came back into the room. "Mr. Heald," the man with the tongs said, "will you kindly identify this?"

Mike stared at it, frowning. "I don't know what it is."

"Oh, come. You had it in your pocket. What's it for?"

"I don't know."

"I don't either, that is, I don't know what it was made for originally, but I'm pretty sure it made a hole in Lawrence's temple and one in Mrs. Fitch's."

"But I don't—I've never—for God's sake!" Mike ran his fingers through his hair. Then he reached for the small object the policeman was handling so carefully.

"Don't touch it," the latter roared and Mike's hand dropped.

At the sound of raised voices Forsyth came out of the bookroom, his eyes moving from the huddled group of police to Mike, staring, white-faced and wild-eyed, at a small object with a sharp end, which was carefully held between tongs.

"What is going on?"

"This, we're practically sure, is the murder weapon that killed Lawrence and nearly killed Mrs. Fitch. It was in Mr. Heald's pocket. He claims he never saw it before. If you'll look closely, that thing that looks like rust on the sharp point is dried blood."

"Mike," Forsyth said, "don't say anything. Cummins will be here any minute."

And then Mike began to laugh. "Hey, give me a fair trial, will you? I remember now where I picked that up."

"I thought you might. Will you come along with us, please?"

"Not without his lawyer," Forsyth said firmly.

Mike grinned, the corners of his mouth turning up steeply. "It's okay. I can't figure out what happened but I know now how I got this and I can guess why Jane was abducted. All my fault."

"And what is it you've just remembered?"

Mike told him.

21

MIKE HAD gone off jauntily between the two policemen and Forsyth was in a flurry of activity. He had a long talk over the telephone with Ralph Cummins and then sent out feelers to learn about the Toyman financial interests and their personal and business bank accounts.

Jane moved restlessly from room to room. A call to the hospital revealed that Mrs. Fitch's condition had deteriorated slightly, though she was in intensive care and everything possible was being done to fan the dim spark of life.

At Jane's request, Mrs. Talent checked on Beverly Barker's alibi. "Though why you should care," the policewoman said.

"Because Chris did so much harm. So terribly much harm. Someone ought to help pick up the pieces."

"My God!" the policewoman ejaculated. But she made the telephone call and then smiled at the anxious girl. "They found her doctor. She wasn't in any shape to commit murder that night or to heave you into a car trunk."

"Well, that's something."

"Look, kid, why don't you relax? So far as you are concerned, it is all over."

"Not if Mike is right. Not if that thing he'd absently dropped into his pocket was one of those bombs from the toy bomber Mrs. Toyman designed, and it killed Chris and nearly killed Mrs. Fitch. Mrs. Toyman loved Chris like a son."

"Not like a son," the policewoman said dryly. "It wasn't the thwarted mother that guy aroused in women. But don't be too hard on her. She's been living in her own hell. Every hour of the day she faces the fact she is responsible for his death." She added thoughtfully, "I wish I could have seen Lawrence. He must have been quite a guy. Four women—that we know of—taken in and their lives mucked up. He certainly got results."

"And now," Forsyth commented as he came into the room, "at twenty-five he is just a statistic. I suppose," he added courteously to Mrs. Talent, "there's no further need for you to stay here."

"I stay until I get orders to leave."

"But with Jane safe—"

"I'm not the only one who counts," Jane said unexpectedly. "What about Mrs. Toyman? Is she safe? If Mike's theory is correct, her husband killed Chris in her presence. She loved him. He can't possibly be sure of keeping her quiet permanently."

"Leave it to the police," Mrs. Talent said. She studied the girl's expression suspiciously. "I mean that. Keep out. You nearly got it once before for interfering."

"You think Mr. Toyman was the whispering voice?"

"So far we've got nothing but speculation and a fancy theory. Could be. But before you go off half-cocked again—" She looked appealingly at Forsyth, who said quickly, "By the way, Jane, the police have come up with a fine record for your friend Stan Wiltshire. Got hold of someone to look at the school records, no easy job in the summertime. He's right at the top of his class, which didn't impress a jury of his peers. Must have made life hell for him. Anyhow he's told them what he knows about the gang that has been terrorizing the south Bronx and they've spread a wide net. Picked up nearly a dozen of these young hoods and put the fear of God into the rest. So you see some good has come out of all this."

Jane clutched at his sleeve. "They won't make him go back there? You're going to help him, aren't you?"

"He is being placed in my custody and he is to see a good plastic surgeon tomorrow. What's more, the doctor's office nurse takes in roomers to eke out her income and she'll be glad to give Stan room and board when he leaves the hospital until he is in shape to face people again. And she is not one to be upset because he is disfigured. So that part is okay, honey. We'll look into the college situation and, if the operation or operations hold him up, arrange for some sort of tutoring."

Jane nodded. "I'm glad. He was so scared and yet he took a chance to save me and he didn't really believe it would be all right for him, between the police and the gang."

"Sometimes," Hilda Talent said, "I get a trifle sick of the juveniles who believe the police are their enemies. They burn down buildings, and destroy property, and mug defenseless people, and then when they are picked up there is a general howl about police brutality and the gentle treatment that should be given to the young. Well, when the young commit adult crimes, they should be treated like adults. I know of cases where there have been a dozen or more convictions and not a single day served in jail. Let them out to do it again." She broke off. "Sorry. I don't usually sound off like that, but the public just sees the young kid looking defenseless. They don't see his victims. They don't know of the growing host of kids who will be fighting the law all their lives and living at the public expense."

Forsyth began to question her about attempts to rehabilitate young habitual criminals and Jane went quietly out of the room and upstairs, where she picked up her handbag, transferring to it the few things she had carried in the shabby old one. She emptied out the coins and bills from the transparent purse, put the bills in a wallet that had her initials in gold. As she did so, she saw a snapshot of Chris, laughing into her face.

Oh, Chris, she said to herself, you've done so terribly much harm, so terribly much. Hurt so many people. She dropped the picture into the wastebasket.

Then she went quietly down the stairs. For a moment she paused, listening for her uncle or the policewoman or Johnson. She could hear her uncle's voice in the bookroom and realized he was on the telephone. He gave an exclamation and broke off to say, "Hundred-dollar bills! From Mrs. Toyman's personal account? I guess that ties it up."

He put down the telephone and the policewoman said, "So we were right. Well, the poor woman made a fool of herself, but I could feel sorry for her. These last few days with her husband needling her about being a mother to that heel and knowing what he had done. God! If I had the choice I'd rather be Mrs. Fitch, who, at least, doesn't know what is happening to her."

Jane slid back the bolt on the door and let herself out. The doorman at the apartment next door glanced inquiringly at her and then raised his whistle. A taxi pulled up and Jane got in, giving him the South Orange address, after an anxious look at her uncle's windows, and shrinking back on the seat.

She wanted to get away at once, but the driver hesitated. "That's a long haul and I don't know if I can pick up anyone coming back."

"I want you to wait for me." As he still hesitated, she looked once more at the windows and opened her purse. "I'll give you twenty on account if you don't trust me."

"Oh, that's okay, lady. So long as I don't have to pile up

mileage without any passenger. Be there long?"

"Probably not more than a few minutes. I don't know."

II

"This the place?" the driver asked dubiously.

The shades had been drawn in the Toyman house and the place had a deserted look. For a moment Jane's heart sank. Perhaps she was too late. Then she saw that the Bentley was parked at the curb.

"She probably pulled down the shades because of the heat," Jane said, speaking to herself.

"Yeah. Will I have time to catch myself some coffee or do you want me to wait here?"

Somewhat to her own surprise Jane heard herself say, "I wish you'd wait." She fumbled in her bag and drew out her wallet, reached over to hand him a twenty-dollar bill. "I don't know—if I'm not out in, say, twenty minutes, I wish you'd call the police."

"Hey, what's going on here?"

"It's probably all right, just a kind of precaution." She pulled out a leather notebook with her initials and wrote her name. "Tell them I came to see Mrs. Toyman about the— the Lawrence case. They'll know."

"Look, lady, I don't want to get mixed up in anything."

"You won't be. Oh, please do as I ask. I may come right out. I just want—to tell her something."

"You carrying a gun?"

Jane laughed and he grinned. "Well, okay, I guess if you say so it's all right. Twenty minutes, huh? And then I call the cops."

She went to the door, pulled the tail of the little dog and heard the barking inside. She waited a long time. She could hear them then, the slow heavy steps on the stairs.

Then the door opened on a chain.

"Who is it?"

"It's Jane Forsyth, Mrs. Toyman."

"I'm awfully sorry, my dear. I can't see you today."

"Please. Just for a minute. There's something I've got to tell you."

There was no answer and the door began to close.

"Wait. Please listen, Mrs. Toyman. The police know—about the money you withdrew from the bank—and the little bomb—and they know Chris must have spoken of that old abandoned house where he stayed for a time when he was broke. So—"

"Oh, for God's sake, go away!"

"But I had to tell you. If your husband—when your husband— Don't you see? You're in danger. Come away with me now. Please, Mrs. Toyman. Come away with me."

The door closed, the chain was released, and the door opened wide. Mrs. Toyman, her face gray, stood back, a look of despair on her face, and Jane entered the house. The door closed behind her and she turned to face Mr. Toyman, looking as though he were ninety, his face unshaven, eyes sunken, lips gray, wearing a bathrobe. She could see the scrawny legs from the knees to the worn bedroom slippers.

"So you figured out that Marge did it," he said. "Poor Marge. I've tried so hard to protect her. Surely you don't intend to destroy her after she's been like a mother—"

The woman whimpered and then, as her control broke, she screamed, "Don't say that again! Don't say that! I can't stand it."

Outside there was the roar of a motor as the taxi took off and Jane's heart sank. He wasn't going to get involved in any fracas; he was getting out. And now no one knew where she was. She should have listened to Hilda Talent. But she had not been able to sit back and let Mrs. Toyman fall into a trap.

"Let's sit down, my dear," Mr. Toyman said and he gestured toward the darkened living room.

"I just—"

"Sit down," he repeated gently, but something in his voice made Jane's eyes leap to his face. He turned to his wife. "You too, Marge."

"Henry, I can't—"

"Sit down. Now then, what's all this about wanting Marge to go away with you?"

Jane was aware of the woman who sat mute, shaking, and knew there was no help from her. Married at twenty to a man old enough to be her father, she had been subjugated all her life. There was no fight in her now. Just that one flash of rebellion when she had seen heaven opening before her, the work she loved and the man she loved. All the romance life had denied her.

Well, Jane told herself, not very truthfully, I'm not afraid of him. Anyhow, what could he possibly do in his own house?

"I thought," she said clearly, "it would be easier for Mrs. Toyman to come to us for a while, so she could escape some of the awfulness when you are arrested."

"Arrested?" The flabby gray lips seemed to tighten. Frail as he was, there was strength in the man, strength of will if not of body. "And what did you tell them, dear Jane?"

"It was Mike. When we came here on Sunday and he was playing with that toy bomber, he dropped one of the bombs into his pocket without realizing it, and it fits the wound on Chris's head and the one on Mrs. Fitch."

"One of those clever little bombs you made, my dear," Toyman said to his wife, who sat and shook and made no comment. "It was bound to turn up somewhere; either Jane or her cousin must have taken it." He turned to his wife. "I'm sorry, my dear. I tried to warn you about those—impulses of yours."

"You aren't going to blame her for what happened," Jane said angrily.

They're only a pack of cards, she told herself. Anyhow I'm young and I'm strong and he's old and feeble and sick. Sick. She looked at him again.

"I don't know what you are trying to do, Jane," Toyman said in a tone of reproach. "If you are suggesting that I had a hand in Chris's death—and he was like a son to me—why, I intended to turn the business over to him."

"No, you didn't. You planned to sell out at a big profit and retire. It was—"

Toyman waited for her to complete the sentence. Mrs. Toyman sat and shook.

Then Toyman said, "I realize how shattered you have been by Chris's death. But these fantasies! Chris and—who else is it I am supposed to have injured?" He smiled. "There's a thing called evidence, you know. The police like evidence. Our laws are based on it."

"But there is evidence," Jane told him.

"Tell me." The gray, flabby lips smiled broadly, revealing shockingly artificial teeth.

"Where Chris is concerned, there is the wound made by one of the little bombs. There is the money Mrs. Toyman withdrew from the bank to give him and which I'll bet you've got in your pocket right now." Toyman made an impulsive gesture with his left hand and winced. "There's an abandoned house where you left me, a house Chris must have told you about."

"And why have I done all these extraordinary things? Marge, what's the name of the doctor who prescribed those sedatives for you a while back? He might be useful to our little Jane."

"You did it because your wife wanted to go on with the business she loved and you wanted to sell out. She wanted Chris for her partner because—"

"She loved him like a son."

Mrs. Toyman whimpered.

"Because she loved him," Jane agreed. "I can understand that."

"Can you indeed?" Toyman shifted his position in the chair. "My poor child, did you tell anyone you were coming here? I really ought to inform your uncle and have him come for you, or that enterprising cousin of yours."

"Of course I told my uncle," Jane said, but there had been a long pause. Too long a pause. "And Mike is with the police this very minute."

"But all you've said applies not to me but to my poor Marge. I've done what I could to protect her from herself, but I can't believe you are so vindictive. You say you understand."

"I believe she is the woman whom Chris registered as Mrs. Carl Lamb. And I can understand that too. She'd made a big decision, but before going on—"

"She wanted to cash in on her investment. Is that what you mean?"

"All right. Maybe she did."

"And the proof of all these fantastic allegations?"

"She wouldn't have killed Chris. Never."

"You're so sure?"

"I'm so sure. And another thing, Mr. Toyman, she'd never have taken back that money. It just isn't in character for her, but for you—it fits like a glove."

There was a pulse beating in his cheek and Jane watched

it with fascinated eyes. "And this woman—what do you call her—"

"Mrs. Harrison Fitch."

"Never heard of her. And why would I want to kill her?"

"I don't know. But when she can talk—"

Again Toyman smiled.

"And even if she can't," Jane cried furiously, "you've got the evidence on you!"

"What do you mean by that?"

"I'll bet anything you've got a bullet hole in your shoulder. That's why you are home today instead of at the shop. You're making Mrs. Toyman nurse you because you're afraid to go to a doctor. And that bullet came from Mrs. Fitch's gun."

"No, Henry, no!" Mrs. Toyman screamed, pulling herself out of her chair, lunging toward him.

He was bending over Jane. He jerked her head back against the chair and raised his right hand in which there was clenched one of the toy bombs with its sharp pointed end.

"Freeze!"

Toyman jerked around like a marionette on a string, staring in disbelief at the two policemen who had come in through the kitchen door with drawn revolvers.

The toy bomb dropped on the carpet, where it was scooped up by one of the men while the other pulled Toyman's hands behind his back and fastened on handcuffs.

Toyman let out a shrill cry of pain.

"Be careful!" Mrs. Toyman called. "The man is hurt. Be careful."

Jane looked at her in wonderment.

"Let's take a look at that shoulder." Over Toyman's protests and his moans of pain, they opened the dressing gown. His scrawny figure was ridiculous in his shorts and T-shirt. His left shoulder was bandaged and blood was seeping through the strapping from the wound which had been opened by the exertions.

One of the men read Toyman his rights.

"What are you going to do to him?" Mrs. Toyman cried.

"We're taking him in, ma'am. Murder One on Charles Lawrence. Murder One on Mrs. Harrison Fitch."

"Murder!" Jane exclaimed.

"She died half an hour ago. Before dying she made a complete statement and signed it before witnesses. She was being blackmailed by Beverly Barker, who really believed she had been supplying money to her so-called husband. Mrs. Fitch wasn't having any. Now she knew she was dying, it didn't matter much, one way or another. She said she got to thinking and realized that of all the people involved there were only four who could have provided the money Lawrence was flashing around: herself, Mr. Forsyth, Lawrence's employer Mr. Toyman, or, more likely, Mrs. Toyman. She understood the woman's point of view. She'd been through it herself. So she figured the whole thing out because she knew Lawrence's ways.

"He'd got money out of Mrs. Toyman and you found out and followed them to the motel. You made her admit you and then you killed him, picked up the money, and got out with your wife. So Mrs. Fitch called you and told you what she suspected. It was supposed to be a quiet meeting but she took a revolver, just in case."

"At least," Mrs. Toyman, said, "let Henry get dressed properly. He can't go out like that. He's very susceptible to colds. I'll go with him. He needs help dressing."

"You just sit still, ma'am, and one of us will help him dress. Joe?"

The other man nodded, his hand closed on Toyman's right arm.

"No!" Toyman cried. "No! It was self-defense. You tell

207

them, Marge. It was self-defense."

"Killing a guy who was half drunk and asleep? Now that's a cute one. Real cute."

"I'm seventy. I'm an old man and I'm tired. I wanted to retire and take it easy. And I had this offer—a terrific offer—"

"Only because I had invented the toys and Chris knew how to put them over. You owed it to me," Mrs. Toyman cried out.

"All right. You got paid for it. And what did I get? A double cross." Toyman was almost screaming. "Marge falls for the young guy and wants to go on in business with him as partner, well more than partner. Chris was to be part of the bargain. So what was to happen to me? Before they could pull a stunt like that, I had to be got out of the way, and Marge was in no mood to wait for me to live out my life." He sniffled in self-pity. "So I had to move first. Self-defense."

"It's true, in a way," Mrs. Toyman said dully. "I guess I just never really put it into words in my own mind."

"Don't talk," Jane cried. "Don't say a word, Mrs. Toyman. My uncle knows a lawyer, Mr. Cummins, who will help you."

The two policemen exchanged glances and one of them went up the stairs, half lifting Toyman along with him, while the latter cried, "It was my business. I'm an old man. They wanted to take everything. They wanted me dead. It was self-defense."

Downstairs Jane and Mrs. Toyman sat in silence. There was nothing left to say. The policeman on guard said sharply, "Here, you all right, miss?"

Jane looked at him blankly and toppled over.

When she opened her eyes, she was lying on the overstuffed couch. The policeman was holding a glass of water to her lips.

"I'm sorry—I just—all of a sudden—"

"You'll be all right now."

"How did you happen to come here? Oh, of course, you were going to arrest Mr. Toyman. Where is he?"

"They've taken him away. Permanently. Found a flock of hundred-dollar bills stuffed in the lining of an old hat. Found a lot more inside his pillowcase. Found Lawrence's keyring and billfold and the rest of the stuff he had in his pockets under the mattress. Probably Toyman thought he could salvage something. Not a man for waste."

"I'll call my uncle. He'll be worried."

The policeman grinned. "We called in. He's about frantic. On his way over here armed with a defense attorney and a policewoman who was supposed to be guarding you. Also a guy named Heald talked to the New York police and they are sending one of their own men."

"But what brought you here?"

"You hired a taxi driver who didn't like the setup and when he heard loud voices, he signaled the first patrol car he could find. That was us. You've got a whole army coming for you, lady."

"And Mrs. Toyman?"

"They took her along. She'll have to stand trial, of course. Accessory after the fact. She stood by while her husband killed a sleeping man. She sure as hell brought the house down around her ears falling for a guy young enough to be her son."

"How could Chris? How could he? And now she has to be punished, as though she hadn't had enough."

"With that guy prompting her there's a chance she might have connived at her husband's murder. Anyhow she don't care any more, ma'am. She just don't care. Now how about your taxi driver? You're running up quite a bill out there."

"Uncle Jim will take care of him. He owes him a lot."

With the policeman's help Jane stood up and, after a moment, nodded. "I'm all right."

Sirens beeped, car brakes screamed to a halt, and before the policeman could get to the door it was flung open and Mike came hurtling through the doorway as though he had been fired out of a gun. He caught Jane in his arms.

"You little fool! You dumb bunny! You nearly got yourself killed. I could kill you myself. Oh, darling, darling!"

The man from the patrol car stood back to admit the invading hordes: two New York detectives, a grim-faced policewoman, and James Forsyth, accompanied by a big impressive man in a beautifully tailored suit.

"I guess," the patrolman said, nodding to his New York colleagues, "I'll get back on the street. I'm not needed here any more." He went out, leaving the door open, and a moment later they heard his voice identifying his car and saying cheerfully, "All clear."